Family Tree

Mary
(b. 1813)

Henry Quiner
(1807–1844)

CAROLINE
(1839–1924)

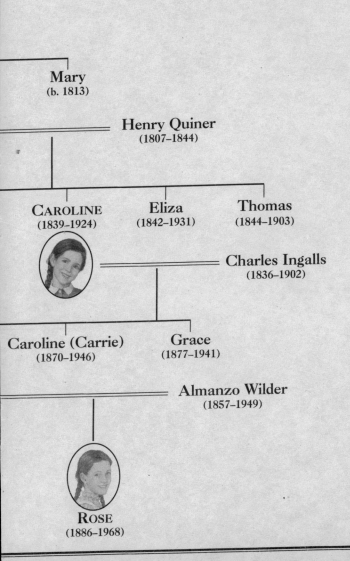

Eliza
(1842–1931)

Thomas
(1844–1903)

Charles Ingalls
(1836–1902)

Caroline (Carrie)
(1870–1946)

Grace
(1877–1941)

Almanzo Wilder
(1857–1949)

ROSE
(1886–1968)

On
Tide Mill Lane

Melissa Wiley

Illustrations by Dan Andreasen

HarperTrophy®
A Division of HarperCollinsPublishers

For Frannie, late but heartfelt

Special thanks to Amy Edgar Sklansky and Diane Hart

Harper Trophy®, ☙®, Little House®, and The Charlotte Years™
are trademarks of HarperCollins Publishers Inc.

On Tide Mill Lane
Text copyright © 2001 by HarperCollins Publishers Inc.
Illustrations copyright © 2001 by Dan Andreasen

Library of Congress Cataloging-in-Publication Data
Wiley, Melissa.
    On Tide Mill Lane / by Melissa Wiley ; illustrations by Dan
Andreasen. — 1st ed.
        p.   cm. — (Little house)
    Summary: Follows the experiences over the course of a year of five-
year-old Charlotte Tucker, who would grow up to become the
grandmother of Laura Ingalls Wilder, living with her family in Roxbury,
Massachusetts, during the war of 1812.
    ISBN 0-06-027013-6 — ISBN 0-06-440738-1 (pbk.)
    ISBN 0-06-027014-4 (lib. bdg.)
    1. Tucker, Charlotte—Juvenile Fiction.   [1. Tucker, Charlotte—
Fiction.   2. Wilder, Laura Ingalls 1867–1957—Family—Fiction.
3. Family life—Massachusetts—Fiction.   4. Massachusetts—History—
War of 1812—Fiction.   5. United States—History—War of 1812—
Fiction.]   I. Andreasen, Dan, ill.   II. Title.   III. Series.
PZ7.W64814 On   2001   00-409002
[Fic]—dc21

6   7   8   9   10
❖
First Harper Trophy Edition, 2001

Contents

On
Tide Mill Lane

The Cornhusking

Darkness had settled upon the house on Tide Mill Lane when Mama and Charlotte and Lydia came out of the lean-to in their everyday bonnets and their warm wool cloaks. Mama carried a pie in a basket over her arm, and baby Mary was snuggled on Mama's hip with the gray cloak tucked up around her. For once Mary did not wriggle to be put down; her face peeped out from the cozy woolen folds. Charlotte and Lydia pulled their cloaks tight at the necks. A cold wind was blowing, a thin persistent wind that slipped in through the crannies and whispered in Charlotte's ears. *Autumn has come*, it said, *winter soon will follow.*

Papa and the boys were just coming out of the barn. In the glow from Papa's lantern Charlotte could see their red noses and ears. Lewis and Tom, her brothers, were blowing on their hands and rubbing them together.

"Whew!" said Papa. "Heath picked a cold night for it, didna he?"

"It'll be warm enough in his barn, with half the town there jawin'," Mama said. "Come, let's get over there before the baby takes a chill."

Papa nodded. "Aye. Carry the pie for ye, shall I?" He helped slide the basket off Mama's arm. With her usual brisk step Mama led the way across the road and past Papa's blacksmith shop and the trees behind it. Charlotte seldom saw the shop like that, with its great wide doors shut and bolted. Papa had closed up a little early tonight, for Mr. John Heath was having a cornhusking.

Mr. Heath's farm was just over the hill, across a stubbly hay meadow and an empty cornfield in which the last dry stalks of corn rattled like paper in the wind. All through August and September the farms around Roxbury had hummed with the work of cutting hay and packing it into barn lofts, and of harvesting the corn and the pumpkins, the oats and the rye, the apples and quince and pears. Now it was time for canning and preserving, husking and storing, making ready for the long, bitter winter. The air held the sharp smell of frost, and the leaves on the maples glowed a red orange as bright as Mama's hair.

Lewis ran ahead through the cornfield, leaping over the tilted stalks, intent on reaching the Heath place first.

"Last one there's a withered ear," he called back over his shoulder.

Tom sprinted to catch up; his breath puffed out in little clouds that hung upon the air. In his bulky woolen coat Tom looked stouter than ever, but he ran swift as a deer when he wanted to. He hardly ever did want to, but he couldn't stand to hear Lewis crowing over winning.

"I don't see why Tom bothers," Lydia said. She was trailing dreamily behind Charlotte, twirling a bit of cornstalk between her fingers. "He can't ever catch up to Lewis. Imagine, a little child not yet eight beating a boy who's going on thirteen."

Mama, striding along beside Papa, turned to look at Lydia.

"Would you listen to that?" Mama teased, "'A little child,' says she. I suppose you think you're quite an auld woman, Miss Lydia— nine years old as you are."

Papa chuckled. "If she's an auld woman, that makes you ancient as the hills, Martha," he said.

Mama snorted. "Ancient I may be, but I could still beat you in a footrace, Lew Tucker."

"I dinna doubt that," Papa said earnestly. His voice was so grave that it made Charlotte laugh. It was strange and exciting to be out after candle time, with the veil of night fallen over the world and the stars piercing the air one by one.

After a while she saw a glow of yellow light over Mama's shoulder—a lantern, hanging in the wide-open doorway of a barn. That was Mr. Heath's barn, and it was full of people.

Voices called out greetings to Mama and Papa. The barn was noisy and warm. A young lady came to Charlotte and kissed her cheek. She was Miss Heath, and she had been Charlotte's teacher last summer. She had pink cheeks and sparkling eyes, and her face was framed with long spiraling curls that had been made with a hot iron rod. Her voice was high and merry. Miss Heath did not seem much like a teacher now. She whirled off to speak to another new arrival, her curls swinging out behind her.

"She's Amelia tonight," Charlotte whispered to Lydia.

"She's always Amelia," said Lydia, confused. "That's her name."

Charlotte didn't try to explain. Lydia was not the sort of person to whom it was easy to explain things.

Mama was; she had a way of seeing at once what you meant when you talked about things like your teacher having a "Miss Heath" self and an "Amelia" self. But Mama was deep in conversation with Mrs. John Heath, who was Miss Heath's mother, of course. Charlotte knew she must not interrupt.

The barn was crowded. On either side of a wide center walkway were great banks of hay stacked from floor to ceiling. Against one of the walls of hay was a mound of corn, hundreds of unhusked ears tumbled together. On the other side was a smaller pile of husked corn, yellow as summer. The earthen floor in between was covered with a pale green carpet of discarded corn husks. And everywhere were people—half the town, indeed, it seemed, just as Mama had said. At any rate, half of the people who were left now that the militia had been called into service. Most of the young men of Roxbury, and many of the fathers, had gone away to defend coastal towns against attacks from the British. Charlotte's own papa would have had to go, if he had not been the town blacksmith. Roxbury could not do without a blacksmith for months on end.

In the big barn, small children ran this way and that, shuffling the corn husks with their feet. Grown-up men and women sat in groups on bales of hay, rapidly stripping the leaves off the ears of corn. Boys dashed up to their sisters and flung fine threads of corn silk into their hair. In one corner stood a cluster of girls busily fashioning dolls out of corn husks and thread.

Mama, still talking to Mrs. Heath, untied her cloak and set Mary down. Mary took off straightaway toward the great pile of corn.

"Watch her, Charlotte," called Mama, laughing. Charlotte hurried after Mary, shrugging out of her own cloak as she went. Mary came to the mountain of corn and crouched down; she took up an ear that was longer than her head and sank her teeth into the raw kernels.

"Mary, no!" Charlotte scolded, trying to wrestle the ear away. The grown-ups all around were chuckling. Mama and Papa sat down on bales of hay and began husking. Mama's slender hands and Papa's big ones flew over the ears of corn, stripping off the green leaves.

Mary was crying for her ear of corn. Charlotte put her arms around the baby's middle and carried her toward the girls making dolls. Lydia was there already. Tom and Lewis had disappeared into the mob of boys. There were so many people in the barn it might as well have been a dance as a husking.

Indeed, across the barn a young man was just jumping onto a bale of hay and lifting a fiddle to his shoulder. A cheer went up from the husking grown-ups. The young man had a wild head of hair cut short in the new fashion. He reminded Charlotte of Will, Papa's striker, who was faraway in the north, marching to Maine with the militia. Charlotte's insides shivered with the cold feeling that came whenever she thought about Will's being gone. She wondered why the fiddler had not gone to war, and guessed that perhaps he was not yet eighteen years old. You had to be eighteen to serve in the militia.

The fiddle music was very loud, but Mary was louder. The baby had forgotten the ear of corn; now she wanted a corn-husk doll. Lydia was making one; she had already tied black thread around one end of a piece of folded corn husk to make a head and neck. Now she was struggling to knot another piece of thread around the waist.

Mary squealed and snatched at the doll.

"Wait till I'm finished," murmured Lydia. Biting her lip, she pulled the knot tight. The doll had corn-husk arms that stuck out stiffly at the sides. Below the black-thread waist, the thick husks made a full skirt that belled out as if there were many petticoats underneath. The doll looked very sweet and dainty, and it would last a long time if it were treated gently. But when Lydia held out the doll, Mary grabbed it and clutched it tightly in her fist, crumpling the pale green skirt.

"Oh, Mary," sighed Lydia. Charlotte put her hand into the pocket of her dress. Her own beloved doll was safe inside, the clothes-pin doll Mama had helped her make on her birthday last spring when she turned five. The doll's name was Emmeline and she had a real painted face, with black eyes and a cheerful red mouth that smiled up at you in the friendliest way.

"Charlotte! There you are," cried a voice. It was Susan, Charlotte's good friend from school. "I've been looking everywhere. I saw your mother and father over there. Your brother put silk in my hair."

"Lewis?"

"No, Tom." Susan was laughing. She didn't mind being "silked." It was part of a husking.

Charlotte helped pick the slippery strands of corn silk out of Susan's fine brown hair. All around them the noise of the husking rose like smoke to the rafters. The fiddle made a merry, rollicking sound. The huskers laughed and chattered and shouted across the barn to each other.

"Amelia's got a red one!" someone cried. A roar of laughter went up from a group of young women and a few young men near the fiddler. Charlotte and Susan ran to watch, for there was always fun to be had when a young lady found red kernels on an ear of corn she had husked.

"Kiss him, kiss him!" Miss Heath's friends were shouting. Sam Dudley, the young man who worked in the tinsmith's shop, grinned and leaned toward Miss Heath, turning his cheek to her expectantly. Miss Heath blushed and dropped a hasty kiss on Sam's cheek. The group of huskers cheered and clapped. Sam's eyes twinkled, and he put a hand to his cheek as if to hold the kiss there. Miss Heath laughed and shook her head.

"Oh, Sam, you are a goose," she teased. But Charlotte could see that Miss Heath was very happy. Everyone knew she was Sam Dudley's sweetheart, and Charlotte had heard Mama say she expected they would marry before the year was out. Sam had not been allowed to serve in the militia because he had injured his back last summer, falling off a horse. He could not walk all the way to Maine with the other soldiers.

Although the huskers were laughing and teasing, they never stopped working, and the green husks fluttered to the barn floor like autumn leaves. Another cry of laughter went up, for one of the young ladies had peeled away the husks to find a withered, shriveled ear of corn inside. That was called a smut ear, and it meant the opposite of a red one.

"Ah, look what Millie's got!" cried the fiddler, whose perch on the hay bale gave him a fine view of the goings-on of his friends. "Hard luck for you, George!"

"Aye, Georgie, step up and take your whipping like a man!"

Charlotte giggled. George Waitt was the apprentice at the gristmill down the lane from her house. Mama had said she suspected George was courting Millie Snyder, and now Charlotte knew it was true. With a mock groan George went to Millie and knelt before her.

"Not again." Millie laughed. "I can't bear to."

"Go on, Millie," coaxed the fiddler. "You know the rules.

> '*The laws of husking every wight can tell—*
> *And sure no laws he ever kept so well;*
> *For each red ear a general kiss he gains,*
> *With each smut ear she smites the luckless*
> *swains.*'

"That's our Georgie-boy, all right, the most luckless swain that ever lived. What does this make, George, the third husking this year with all smut ears and no red?"

"The fourth," lamented George. "I'm beginning to fear someone is planting the smut ears against me on purpose."

"Aye, Millie's father most likely!" said one of the young men slyly, and another roar of laughter went up from the merry group. Charlotte and Susan were watching with delight. These young men and women were very nearly old enough to be mothers and fathers themselves, but when they met at a husking they were as naughty and teasing as little boys and girls. Black-haired Millie shrugged apologetically and smacked George on the shoulder with the withered ear of corn. George gave a mock wince, and Millie giggled. As George stripped his next ear, he pretended to quake with fear. But this one was not withered.

The mountains of husked corn grew higher and higher, and the pile of unhusked corn had shrunk to a mere hill. Mr. Heath's barn was like a range of mountains, with the great high banks of hay on both sides reaching the cobwebby rafters, and the corn hills of various sizes. Charlotte threw back her head and spun around to see the landscape of hay and corn and people whirl past. Susan whirled around, too, and when Mary saw them she left Lydia and came to clutch at Charlotte's skirt until Charlotte took her baby sister's hands and helped her dance in circles.

After a while they were all very dizzy. Mama came over to take Mary; she said Charlotte and Susan ought to go and rest in the hay before they made themselves sick. So Charlotte took Susan's hand and together they stumbled toward one of the great golden heaps and flung themselves into it.

The hay made a springy, prickly, sweet-smelling bed. Charlotte lay looking up at the rafters wheeling around above her. The tin lanterns hanging on the rope above the barn floor seemed to soar in trails of light, like shooting stars.

Stars made her think of Will. Papa had said that sometimes the soldiers camped in tents, and other times, on fine nights, they slept beneath the stars. Charlotte wanted to know what it was like to sleep outside, with the earth for your bed and the night sky for your coverlet. She guessed it would be terribly cold, not cozy like snuggling up next to Lydia under a heavy quilt, or like lying here on a cushion of hay in the warm and crowded barn. But she would like to look up at the stars. It was something, if Will had the sky and stars and moon to keep him company away up there in the cold north where men

15

were fighting battles for reasons that made no sense to Charlotte.

The savory smell of chicken pie came into the barn. Mama and Mrs. Heath and some of the other ladies were setting out dishes of food upon a table made of a long wooden plank set upon two short logs. Charlotte sat up, blinking; she had begun to feel sleepy lying in the grassy bed. Now the good smells of baked beans and potatoes and boiled pumpkin woke her back up. The huskers were working quickly to finish the last ears of corn. The fiddler had already put down his fiddle, so as to be first in line at the table.

Charlotte and the other children crowded close to look at the food. There was Mama's pear pie, with the crisscrossing strips of golden crust upon the top. Charlotte's mouth watered just looking at it. Everyone said Mama made the best pear pie in Roxbury. There was apple pie, too, that someone else had made, and a great orange mound of mashed sweet potatoes in a glazed clay crock, and a heaping platter of steamed clams that smelled like a salt breeze blowing across South Boston Bay.

Mama had said that morning that Thanksgiving was coming soon. Tom had whooped, for he loved to eat, and Mama's Thanksgiving feast was so sumptuous that every year the table nearly broke beneath it. But Charlotte thought a husking was very nearly as nice as Thanksgiving Day. You were not given as much food on your plate (for though Mrs. Heath's makeshift table was loaded, there were a great many mouths to feed), but there was the fiddling and the dancing and the grown-ups playing games. You could eat laughter and drink music, and Charlotte thought that no matter how much of them she had, she never would feel too full.

In Town

Suddenly husking time was over, and Thanksgiving Day came, with its good smells and groaning table. Mama baked for a week, getting ready for the feast, and on Thanksgiving morning she was up long before dawn, chopping and boiling and mashing. She had bought a goose from a farmer out on the Brookline Road. Charlotte and Lydia helped to pluck it. They saved the feathers in a linen sack, for stuffing into pillows later.

Then came the flurry of picking feathers

out of one another's hair and rushing into Sunday dresses. It was not a Sunday, but Thanksgiving Day was a go-to-meeting day nonetheless. Charlotte tried not to fidget on the pew, but the Reverend Mr. Tubbs spoke a very long time, and the thought of roast goose was very loud in her stomach.

At last the minister had said his final "amen," and the eager crowds burst out of the meetinghouse into the crisp air. Charlotte ran to greet Susan and some other children she knew from school, and there was just time for a quick game of Milking Pails before their mothers called them all to go home.

"Will you buy me a pair of milking pails,
Oh, mother! Oh, mother?
Will you buy me a pair of milking pails,
Oh, gentle mother of mine?

Where is the money to come from,
Oh, daughter, oh, daughter?
Where is the money to come from,
Oh, gentle daughter of mine?"

They could play games that day, because it was not a Sunday. It felt naughty to run around shouting right after church, but it wasn't, because it was Thursday. Charlotte ran so hard that she could not stop running when Mama called her, and so she ran all the way down Washington Street toward home. Tom and Lydia ran with her. Lewis passed them all, calling out, "How many pies d'you think I can eat before the rest of you get home?"

That made Tom put on a burst of speed, and he caught up with Lewis at the corner of Tide Mill Lane.

All the rest of that day was for laughing and eating. Charlotte counted fourteen different kinds of food on the table. Papa said the blessing, thanking God for the bountiful feast and for the good health the whole family had enjoyed in the past year. Breathing in the rich smell of roast goose, Charlotte felt thankful down to the tips of her toes. She ate three helpings of goose and half the goose liver. Charlotte and Lewis were the only two children who liked goose liver, so Mama let them share it between them.

When everyone had eaten so much that no one could move from the table, Mama ladled out mugs of steaming hot cider, spiced with cinnamon and cloves. While they all sipped their cider, with the warm spicy steam enveloping their faces, Mama told stories. She made them all laugh till their stomachs ached with the tale of the nearsighted old man who came upon a cow in a pasture, mistook it for his horse, and tried to ride it home.

That was Thanksgiving, and it was a delicious day in every respect.

When the cold north winds of December brought winter to Roxbury, the big boys and girls went to school. Lydia and Lewis and Tom all went, but Charlotte did not go. She was only five and a half, and that was not old enough for the winter school. Mama said she was glad. She liked to have Charlotte's company about the house.

A few last brown, tattered leaves clung to the bare branches of the oak trees behind the house on Tide Mill Lane. Mama had a fire going in the parlor almost all the time now, and of course the kitchen hearth was always bright with flames. Charlotte was kept busy all day long, running out to the lean-to for a few sticks of wood. She helped look after Mary, too, to make sure the baby did not get into the fire.

Charlotte loved to have Mama almost all to herself on the quiet winter mornings, when the older children were away in the schoolhouse having to sit still and silent for fear of the schoolmaster's cane. The winter-term schoolmaster was not kind and jolly like Miss Heath, who taught the younger children in the summer term. Charlotte thought she'd rather skip winter school forever and stay home instead to help Mama bake and sew and spin, even if it meant chasing Mary away from the fire a hundred times a day. Mama's quick laugh and quick hands made the house seem light and lively even when the world outside was gray and dull as clouds.

Sometimes Mama put on her cloak and

bonnet and said, "Come, lassies, let's do us some marketin'." Then Charlotte would rush for her own cloak and for Mary's little coat and hood. Mama would take down a wide-bottomed straw basket in which to carry things home, and Charlotte had a little basket of her own with a bit of black ribbon tied around the handle.

One morning Mama said Charlotte's little basket was the only basket they would need.

"You shall be my strong arm, Lottie," Mama said.

They went out through the lean-to, through the front dooryard, and across the road to the smithy. Mama stopped in the doorway of the crowded shop to wave a cheerful hello to Papa, who was bent over his anvil hammering a curved piece of iron with a small mallet. Papa looked up and smiled, but he did not stop his work. He was very busy these days, with Will gone to fight the British and the boys in school.

Mama said Papa would most likely have to hire another striker to help him out until

Will came back. No one knew when that would be; the war had already been going on for more than two years, ever since the spring of 1812. Now 1814 was coming to a close, and still the British ships reigned in Boston Harbor, and the fierce British army held fast against the American troops in the north.

Papa's shop was always full of farmers and townsmen who gathered to talk about the war. It was full today, and Charlotte saw one man wave a newspaper in the air, saying, "It's my opinion this fella here has it right—New England ought to put her foot down and refuse to have anything more to do with this durned war. Just you wait till the Hartford Convention commences next week, and then we'll see some bold action. I hope they vote to tell the War Department to go sit in a durned lake!"

Papa turned from his work and stood up very straight. He gave the man a long, quiet look with upraised eyebrows. The man's eyes glanced toward the doorway where Mama and the girls were standing, and he blushed and stammered an apology.

"Beg pardon, ma'am, I didn't see you there. I hope you'll forgive my language, old cuss that I am."

"The vulgarity I could forgive," said Mama tightly. "But I'll not stand for talk of treason."

The man's eyebrows went up. He said to Papa, with a little mocking laugh, "I see your wife's the outspoken sort, eh, Tucker?"

"My wife," said Papa in a dangerous tone, "is right, Bert. Unless ye'd care to hoof it all the way to Dorchester for your ox chains, ye'll mind what ye say in my shop."

The man named Bert shifted uncomfortably, scowling at the forge.

"And if that paper you're waggling is the *Centinel*," Mama added, "you'd do better to read the label on a bottle of snake oil. That rag is pure poison."

The other men were watching this exchange in careful silence. Their glances went back and forth between Mama's blazing eyes and Bert's smoldering gaze.

"All right," said Bert at last. "My mother didn't raise the sort of fella who'd cause a woman grief on *her husband's* own land."

His eyes narrowed when he said that, and Mama's lips were thin and white.

"I've got business t'other side of Great Hill," Bert added. "I reckon I'll stop by here for my chains on the way back. Good day, ma'am." His voice was cold.

Mama ushered Charlotte aside to let the man pass through the doorway. He took a few steps toward the street, and then he turned back, holding up the newspaper.

"I'm not the only man feels this way, you know. There's a good many of us, and the governor's one of 'em."

He walked away quickly, stuffing the paper in his pocket.

"Aye, and there's a thing or two I'd like to say to the governor, if I had the chance," said Mama, looking at Papa.

Papa grinned wryly.

"*Only* one or two things, Martha?"

That set the other men laughing, and

Mama smiled. "Well, to start out with. I wouldn't want to frighten the man."

"And you could do it, too, Mrs. Tucker," called out one of Papa's customers.

"Aye," said Papa, "my wife could frighten the president."

"Och, go on with ye," Mama scolded. There was laughter in her voice now. All the anger Charlotte had felt radiating off Mama while Bert was in the shop seemed to have blown away.

"Come, Charlotte," said Mama, "we'll never get our errands done at this rate. Mary, do leave off pullin' on my bonnet strings!"

Another burst of laughter followed them out the door. Charlotte caught Mama's hand and skipped beside her. They came to the corner of Washington Street, the wide main street of Roxbury. If you followed it far enough, you would go all the way to Boston. Charlotte knew, for she had gone almost that far by herself. But Mama and Charlotte had no need to make the long walk to Boston today along the lonely, windswept road people called "the Neck." They were bound for Mr. Stock's shop on Union Street.

"Your father's new hat ought to be ready by now," Mama said. "But dinna you say a word to him about it unless he asks, Lottie. I'm just going to put the new one on the peg and hide the old one away, and we'll see how long it takes him to notice."

Charlotte laughed, but Mama said, "Think it's funny, do you? I'm not after playin' a joke on him, you know—I simply canna think o' another way to get him to keep the new hat! What I'm hopin' is that he willna notice for a few days, and by then 'twill be too late to take it back. Your father is the kindest, dearest man that ever lived, Lottie, but when it comes to spendin' money on himself he's the stubbornest there ever was, too. That old hat o' his is a disgrace. I've been after him to replace it these past two winters gone. I think if 'twere left up to him, he'd wear it until his head poked clean through the crown! And then he'd only say, 'Och, Martha me dear, I'm after needin' a tiny wee patch on me lid.'"

In Town

Mama sounded exactly like Papa when she said that.

"Say some more, Mama," Charlotte begged, but Mama shook her head.

"Nay. Enough is as good as a feast," she said.

They passed the gristmill where Mr. Waitt, the miller, ground wheat and rye and oats into flour. They passed the potter's shop with its funny hive-shaped kiln in which old Mr. Hubbard baked his clay pots to make them hard and waterproof. They crossed the wooden plank bridge over Stony Brook, the bubbling creek that flowed down from the marshlands known as the Roxbury Flats, which were in turn fed by the tidal surges of the great Charles River.

Past Stony Brook, the road turned, and Charlotte saw the church spire rising above the town common. The common was an open, grassy place between two busy streets: Washington Street on one side, and Dudley Street, where white-columned mansions rose aloofly above clipped boxwoods, on the other.

The mansions were quiet, but the streets were lively with people and dogs and oxcarts. A crowd of men stood talking on the steps of the town hall. Six or seven sheep were grazing on the short, withered grass of the common. A small boy rolled a wooden hoop onto the grass and chased after it, scattering the sheep. His mother hurried after him, scolding.

On the way to Union Street they stopped at the tinsmith's shop to buy a nutmeg grater. The old one's points were so worn down that it would no longer grate the hard nutmegs. Mama let Charlotte put the three copper pennies onto Mr. Hunt's counter, and it was Sam Dudley who solemnly took them and counted them into his money box. He wrapped up the grater in a piece of brown paper and held it out to Charlotte. Mama told Charlotte she might carry the grater in her own basket. With the grater inside, the basket pulled on Charlotte's arm in a satisfying way. It felt very grown-up to pay for a nutmeg grater herself and to feel its solid weight in her pretty ribboned basket.

The tinsmith's shop was the first in a row of shops that ran along Washington Street, facing the busy common. The shops' doors were closed against the frosty December air. In summer, when the doors were always wide open, Charlotte liked to look inside each shop as she and Mama passed. She liked to see the rows of goods for sale and the mysterious equipment with which the craftsmen plied their various trades.

But even with the doors closed she could tell what went on inside by the signs hung over the doorways. A wooden hoop—that was the cooper's shop, with the row of stout barrels lined against the wall like well-fed soldiers, and dozens upon dozens of differently sized hoops hanging on pegs above them, and the thick, fragrant carpet of sawdust on the floor that crunched softly when you stepped on it.

Next was the printer's shop, with printed notices stuck up all over the door, and a bundle of newspapers tied up with string sitting on the doorstep. The corners of the top papers were ruffling in the breeze. Charlotte could smell the ink inside the shop. A large building with glass windows and a green canvas awning was the tavern. Its sign brandished a mug on a dinner plate with a knife on one side and a fork on the other. A group of muddy-booted men, smelling of smoke and cider, was coming out the door. A hubbub of voices rumbled out of the tavern behind them.

The men with muddy boots passed by without seeming to notice Mama and Charlotte and Mary. Only one of them tipped his hat and bowed to Mama. Charlotte watched them climb into a pair of wagons that were parked beside the tavern. A fourth man, his boots just as travel stained, was checking the harnesses on the team of horses that belonged to one of the wagons. The wagon boxes were piled high with cider barrels and sacks of meal. Charlotte knew the men were teamsters, for she had seen many a team stop at Papa's smithy for repairs to their wagons. The teamsters hauled supplies in and out of Boston.

After the tavern came an open lot, and then a pine building with a flat wooden hat hanging over the door. That was the hatmaker's shop. Mama pushed open the red door and ushered Charlotte inside.

Mr. Stock, the hatmaker, was a stout man with bushy eyebrows and side-whiskers and a thick, wavy mass of hair the color of cold ashes. His shop was small, little more than a row of shelves, a wide counter littered with hat frames and tools, a hearth, and a bit of open space for customers to stand in. The portly hatmaker stood behind his counter, stretching a circle of wet felt over a rounded wooden frame. His eyes looked up when Charlotte and Mama came inside, but his hands went on smoothing and pulling at the felt.

"Good day, Mrs. Tucker," he said. His voice was deep and rough at the edges. "Wondered if we'd see you today."

Mary was wriggling in Mama's arms. Mama put her down and told Charlotte to keep a close eye on her. Charlotte took Mary's hand—Mary liked to walk with Charlotte that way, sometimes. They walked to the end of the high counter and peeked around it at the rows and rows of shelves. The shelves were full of hats, all kinds of hats. Black ones, brown ones, gray ones; men's hats with wide brims and low crowns or narrow brims and high crowns. There were hats with ribbons round them and hats with feathers stuck in their bands. There were women's bonnets, with wide, curving brims and wax fruit stuck on top. But there were only a few women's hats. Mostly the hats were for men, and Charlotte stared at them, trying to guess which one was for Papa.

"Mr. Tucker's hat is ready, then?" Mama asked Mr. Stock.

He grunted. From a high shelf he took down a crisp new hat. It was bowl shaped, with a flat brim, made of stiff, black felt. It was very plain, and Charlotte hadn't noticed it among the others.

"This will last your husband a good long while," said Mr. Stock. "You can't beat beaver felt for durability. Worth the extra cost."

Mama turned the hat over and looked inside. She ran her finger around the leather sweatband sewn around the crown.

Mary pulled on Charlotte's hand. She wanted to go behind the counter to play with the things on the lower shelves. Those were Mr. Stock's work shelves, and they were scattered with tools and brushes, spools of ribbon, and strips of leather. There were more of the wooden, head-shaped hat frames, a whole army of them in different sizes. Charlotte thought they looked like a family of wooden-headed people, or dolls waiting to have eyes and mouths painted on.

"No, Mary, don't touch," she said, although she'd have liked to play with the hat frame family, too. Mr. Stock glanced down at Charlotte and Mary beneath his bristling eyebrows. Mary shrank back against Charlotte's skirt, and Charlotte led her back to Mama.

"Yes, this will do nicely," Mama was saying. She took several coins out of her pocketbook and placed them upon the counter. "You do fine work, Mr. Stock."

"Thank'ee, ma'am," Mr. Stock grunted. He slid the coins into his hand and deposited them somewhere behind the counter. Then he put Papa's hat inside a tall brown box with a string attached. He lifted the box by the string and handed it to Mama.

With the hatbox dangling off her arm, Mama scooped up Mary and said good-bye to Mr. Stock. He was already back at work smoothing the wet piece of felt over the big hat frame on his counter. Charlotte wondered who that hat was for, and whether she would recognize it if she saw it on someone's head.

"Come along, Lottie," Mama said, pulling open the door.

A rush of cold wind swept into the shop. It smacked into Charlotte's face, making her eyes sting. Mama shivered and tucked her cloak tight around Mary.

"Och, let's hurry ourselves home," Mama said. "I wanted to stop at Bacon's for some candlewicking, but I'll not keep Mary out in this cold. This wind certainly blew in out of nowhere. Here, let me tie your hood, Lottie."

The icy wind pushed at Charlotte all the way home. The sheep were gone from the common; probably they had wandered home to the shelter of their own barn. Mama said there must be a storm blowing down from the north.

"Where Will is?" asked Charlotte, for she thought of him whenever someone spoke of the north.

"Happen so," said Mama. "But I hope not. I dinna like to think o' those poor boys sleepin' out in the open with naught but a sheet o' canvas between them and the cold. I thank the Lord your brother Lewis wasna old enough to join up."

"When will the war end, Mama?" asked Charlotte.

"I canna say, lass. President Madison is doin' his best to bring the British to their senses, I'll give him that much. He sent some o' his best men over there to discuss callin' off the fightin'. But these things take time."

The nutmeg grater in Charlotte's basket

bumped up and down as she hurried alongside Mama toward Tide Mill Lane. All the
way along Washington Street she was thinking
of the things being made behind the closed
doors: wool hats and tin nutmeg graters and
horseshoes; barrels and wagon wheels and
newspapers that told about the war.

The Letter

One day Mama kept Lewis home from school to run errands and split wood. She sent him to Mr. Bacon's general store on Union Street to buy candlewicking and a jar of peppercorns and a paper of pins. He came back with all that and more, for Mr. Bacon was also postmaster and had given him a letter for Papa.

It was a battered, stained letter with the wax seal half broken off. Mama studied the smudged writing on the front and said, "I know this hand. 'Tis from our Will. Lewis,

40

run and fetch your father from the shop."

Charlotte jumped up and down. A letter from Will!

But Lewis said, "Papa's not there, Mama. He went out to the Craft farm to shoe horses."

"Och," said Mama, vexed. She sighed regretfully. "We'll have to wait till he comes in for dinner, then."

She set the letter on the top shelf of the sideboard. Charlotte saw how often Mama's eyes glanced back at the shelf as she went about her work, and she knew that Mama was impatient to open it, too.

The kitchen was wonderfully warm that day, for it was a baking day. Mama had built a fire in the brick oven when she first got up, and all the long morning delicious things had gone in and out of the oven. Two loaves of bread sat cooling in the pantry, and now a nearly baked sponge cake was filling up the kitchen with its sweet smell.

Mama moved swiftly about the kitchen, getting dinner ready. She sliced half a dozen onions and dropped them into a pot of boiling water that hung from the iron arm of the fireplace crane. Another pot, this one filled with pieces of yellow squash, hung beside it. Mama rolled out a pie crust, and since Mary was napping in the big parlor bed and therefore needed no looking after, Mama said Charlotte might tuck the bottom crust into the pan.

"What kind of pie, Mama?" Charlotte asked, climbing onto a stool at the long table in the middle of the kitchen.

"Pork. Mr. West from the Brighton Road butchered a pig last week and paid your father in pork for smith work."

Charlotte's heart galloped. A pork pie *and* a letter from Will—such a day!

When the bottom crust was in place, Mama laid slices of the fresh pork upon it. Then she sliced a peeled apple onto the layer of pork. More pork, another layer of apple slices, and then Charlotte was allowed to sprinkle the brown sugar and allspice over the pie. Mama gently set the top crust in place and cut three slits in it with a knife to allow the steam to escape during baking.

Out came the sponge cake from the oven, and in went the pork pie. The sweet, golden smell of the cake mingled with the fragrances of stewing onions and bubbling squash. Soon the pork pie began to emit its own rich and savory aroma. The assault of good smells made Charlotte feel wild with hunger. But she was hungriest of all for Will's letter.

As she worked, Mama was singing:

"O, Charlie is my darlin',
My darlin', my darlin',
O, Charlie is my darlin',
The young chevalier!"

With "chevalier" Mama took up the linen towel she used to protect her hand from burning and took the iron door off the brick oven. The good smell of the pork pie nearly made Charlotte dizzy. Mama drained the water from the onion pot and the squash. She stirred a little milk into the onions and dropped a dollop of butter into the bright squash. Then she seasoned both dishes with salt and pepper, and she told Charlotte to step lively and set the table.

At last dinner was on the table and Papa's boots were clomping on the lean-to floor beside the water basin. The sound of Lewis's hatchet had ceased outside the kitchen window. Papa came in, rubbing his clean hands to dry them, with Lewis just behind. Papa's face was red from the scrubbing he had given it, but his hair was dusty with soot. Blacksmithing was sooty work.

Before Papa had half crossed the kitchen, Mama had Will's letter down off the shelf and was thrusting it into Papa's hands.

"Read it now, won't you, Lew? That pie'll keep warm another minute."

Papa's eyes twinkled. "Well now, I dinna ken. A man gets mighty hungry poundin' iron all mornin'—"

"Lew!"

Now Papa's whole face was grinning. "All right, Patience," he teased. Lewis and Charlotte burst out laughing, for it was a double joke. Patience was the name of one of Mama's cows.

But Charlotte was glad Mama was impatient to open the letter. She felt sorry for Lydia and Tom, eating their cold dinners at their benches in the schoolhouse beneath the watchful eye of the master. They were missing out on both the pork pie and Will's letter. But Charlotte didn't feel so sorry that she wanted to wait for them. There would be leftover pie warmed up at suppertime, and Will's letter once opened could be read again and again.

Papa had broken the seal and was unfolding the paper. Charlotte caught a glimpse of writing on the front, sprawling lines and loops of it, and something else besides. There were drawings on the paper, a large bird in a top corner and a little animal, Charlotte couldn't tell what, at the bottom.

Mama crowded close to Papa, reading, and Lewis crowded him from the other side. Papa laughed and gave Mama the letter altogether.

"You read it," he said.

"Dear Mr. Tucker," Mama began,

"It is with great pleasure I take pen in hand to inform you and your family of my health. As yet I have encountered no danger greater than the threats posed to my ears by the thunderous snores of my tentmates. As mine are ears long accustomed to the noises of the forge and hammer, you will agree that the deafening quality of the snoring is truly a marvel of nature.

"Here are some drawings for the little ones. An owl I saw sitting on the ridgepole of a barn as if he owned it, and a chipmunk for Charlotte. It was sitting on a fence nibbling an acorn the way you'd eat an ear of corn.

"We march from dawn to dusk, almost. The weather grows increasingly bitter. Our lieutenant is a good fellow, solid and strong. He does not lord it over his troops as some officers do. He has served under Major General Richardson before this and was none too pleased when Richardson was dispatched to Portsmouth and Lieutenant Colonel Stark placed in command in his stead. Stark is regular army, and a lot of

our militia boys went about swearing they'd not take orders from a regular. I guess someone complained loud enough to Boston, for Stark is gone and our old friend Richardson is back in command.

"As for me, I'm content to put one foot before the other and see what the road brings me to. They have some glorious country up here, let me tell you. I have seen—"

Here Mama turned the paper over to read the other side. Charlotte stood below and looked up at the drawing of the owl on the front of the letter. Tufted feathers stood up at the sides of its head like alertly pointing ears. Its round eyes seemed to stare right down at Charlotte in a hungry way that made her feel she might have been a fat little mouse.

"I have seen some fine sights," Mama continued.

"A bald eagle swooping down and snatching a rabbit right out from under Joshua Frisbee's nose, almost. Josh had just brought the rabbit down and was setting up a hoorah about

having some fresh meat that night. Then this old eagle just hooks it and flies off with it, calm as you please. I'd swear the old bird was laughing at him.

"Last night I saw a couple of moose tussling by the river. You can't imagine how big they are. Paper is hard to come by so I'd best not take the room to show you what they looked like. I know your little shavers would like to see them, though.

"You must excuse me for not writing often as paper truly is scarce. Of course I write my mother and father when I can, and you can get news from them. Please remember me to them and also to Miss Lucy Keator. Did Sam Dudley get up the nerve to ask Miss Amelia Heath's hand yet? Someone ought to give him a shove toward the minister.

"My sincere respects to you and to Mrs. Tucker and to all your young ones. Your friend,

Will Payson"

"That boy missed his calling, Lew," Mama

said. "Look at these drawings. He ought to have been a painter, like my brother Duncan."

"He's a fine smith, though," Papa said. Since Will left he had often said he hated to hire someone in his place. Lewis was trying hard to fill Will's shoes, but a boy of thirteen could not wield the heavy hammers that shaped and pounded the red-hot iron into tools and kettles and chains. And Papa would not let Lewis miss school this winter. He said he wanted his sons to have all the education they could. Even today, Lewis would have to go to school after dinner, now that Mama's errands were done.

Mama let Charlotte hold the letter. The owl and the chipmunk looked so real it seemed they might leap off the page. Charlotte hadn't known Will could draw like that.

"Let me see it," Lewis urged, pulling the paper away from Charlotte.

She let go hastily for fear it would tear but cried out angrily, "I wasn't finished looking!"

Mama said they must all be finished for now or their dinner would be stone cold.

Hungry as she had been, Charlotte hardly tasted the pork-and-apple pie now. She wished Will had been able to draw the moose in the river; she wanted very much to see what a moose looked like. She wished she could go to Maine, too. She had never even been to Boston yet. Papa said the place where Will was now was more than a hundred times farther away than Boston.

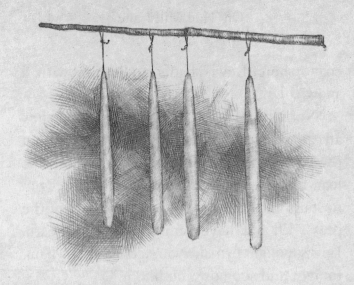

Candle Making

In the middle of December, the first snow came. It was a heavy, wet kind of snow that stuck to Mama's shoulders when she came in from feeding the hens their breakfast and made her hands shiny wet when she tried to brush herself off. The snow fell all of one whole day, and it was still falling thickly when Lewis and Lydia and Tom came in from school. Snow stuck to their hats and coats; it clung to their boots. Even their eyelashes had snowflakes melting on them. Tom had snow all down his back, inside his coat, where Lewis had caught him with a snowball.

"Not a step farther," Mama said when they all came crowding into the warm kitchen from the lean-to. She made them go back into the lean-to to shake off the snow. "Charlotte, run upstairs and fetch Tom a new shirt out of the press. I'll not have him catchin' his death. Lewis, I ought to make you sleep in a snowbank tonight and see how you like it."

Charlotte hurried upstairs. The upper story was cold. Mama kept the kitchen and parlor fires burning all day, but she only kindled a fire in Charlotte and Lydia's bedroom when she wanted to weave at the big loom across from their beds. The boys' room did not even have a fireplace. Charlotte could see her breath in the air when she went in to get Tom's dry shirt. She did not like to stay in that room a moment longer than she had to.

Coming into the kitchen was like passing through a curtain of heat. Mama hung a kettle of cider over the fire to warm. She made Tom sit wrapped in a blanket beside the hearth, to make sure he did not catch a chill. Tom sat hunched and swathed, glaring out from the folds of the blanket at Lewis. Lewis, grinning broadly, sat leaning back in a chair with his arms behind his head, to show how freely he could move. Then Mama scolded him for tipping the chair and set him to work peeling potatoes, and it was Tom's turn to grin.

"If this storm keeps up, I'll not send you to school tomorrow," Mama said.

"I hope it never stops," said Lydia. "I hate that Master Phelps. I don't care if I never see him again."

"Lydia!" Mama said sharply. "None of that. 'Hate' is an ugly word and makes them ugly who use it."

"But, Mama," Lydia protested, "I thought you didn't like Master Phelps either! You told Papa he ought to be run out of town."

"Aye, I did, and I meant it. I don't hold wi' whippin' a child for spellin' 'city' with an *s*, as he whipped Jonas Dudley. I think you could throw a stone in Boston and knock down a dozen schoolteachers better than Otis

Phelps. But that still doesn't give you leave to *hate* him, or anyone else."

Lydia went to the looking glass on the kitchen wall and stared at her reflection, her eyes crinkled in worry.

"Does hate really make you ugly, Mama?" she asked, touching her nose as if she expected it to begin growing longer at any second.

Lewis guffawed.

"She means it makes you ugly *inside*," he said. Charlotte nodded; even she had understood what Mama meant. She wondered how on earth it was that Lydia could be so much older than she was and not understand the simplest things.

But Lydia had her own way of understanding things. She was not a good pupil, like Lewis and Tom. Tom had told Charlotte that Lydia was at the foot of her class. She stumbled over her spelling, and she was hopeless at arithmetic. She could not remember any of the principal cities of Europe.

But Mama's sheep came to Lydia when she

called them, and Lydia had been able to milk the cows all by herself since she was eight. Both of Mama's cows stood perfectly still when Lydia milked—not just calm Mollie, but even the twitchy, misnamed Patience, who had stepped on Mama's foot more than once. Mama said it was uncanny the way Lydia could charm an animal.

Lydia had the same knack with babies, too. She could keep Mary entertained for hours at a stretch. Mary was a year and a half old now, and she had learned how to say no. She said it to Charlotte often, her round little face drawn in an expression that was sterner than Mama's very sternest look. It made Charlotte laugh, and then Mary would grow sterner still. But she was never stern with Lydia. Whenever Lydia came in from school, Mary ran to meet her with outstretched arms. She spent half her day riding on Lydia's hip or cuddling in Lydia's lap. Mama often said she didn't know what she'd do without Lydia, for Mary was a handful.

Lydia was still staring into the looking

glass. Droplets of melted snow glistened in the soft fringe of hair on her forehead. Mama told her to come and drink some of the hot cider, to take away the snow's chill.

The snowstorm did last through the night. The next day it was not falling quite so heavily, but still it was falling and the bitter night wind had turned a lot of it to ice. Papa had to open and close the lean-to door over and over, pushing it hard against the piled-up snow, before it would open far enough for him to squeeze himself through. He used Mama's ash shovel to clear a path across the road to the smithy. Mama said she would certainly not have the children fight their way to school through such snow.

"You boys may go to the shop wi' your father," she said at breakfast, and Lewis whooped with pleasure. Lydia cheered, too, for she was glad to miss a day of Master Phelps's lessons.

But then Mama said, "It's an ill wind that blows no good. It's high time we got to the candle making, anyway. We'll start as soon as breakfast is cleared away."

Then Lydia sighed, for she hated careful work like candle making. But Charlotte was glad. She liked to help, and Mama said she was good at it. Last year she had been only four years old, but she had dipped more candles than Lydia, and better ones, too. Mama said it took a steady hand and a patient heart to make a good candle. Lydia had patience for animals and babies, but not for candles.

When Papa and the boys were gone, the breakfast dishes washed and wiped, and the beds made upstairs and down, Mama took out the big crock of tallow she had saved all through the fall. Tallow was animal fat, the grease that ran out of pork and bacon and beef when Mama cooked them. In the pan the grease was wet and shiny, but after Mama had poured it into the tallow crock and let it cool, it became hard and waxy, just right for candles.

Mama put the crock over hot coals so that the tallow would begin to melt. She filled her big iron cauldron half full of water and hung it over the fire to boil. While she waited for the water to bubble, she took the ash shovel and pulled out a heap of white-hot embers onto the stone flooring of the hearth. She placed some andirons over the embers and, when the water was boiling, moved the heavy cauldron to rest on the andirons above the hot coals.

The melting tallow was beginning to smoke, so Mama took the crock and set it right inside the cauldron of hot water. The water lapped at the sides of the crock but didn't rise high enough to spill into the tallow. The hot water would finish melting the tallow.

All this time, Charlotte and Lydia had been putting candlewicks onto the dipping rods. Mama had cut the wicks earlier from the length of hemp string Lewis had brought home from Mr. Bacon's store. Each wick was a long piece of twisted string with a loop at one end. Charlotte and Lydia slid the loops onto straight, slender sticks that Mama had saved from last year. The sticks were the dipping rods, and there were four or five wicks to a rod.

"Lydia, you mind the baby while Charlotte and I dip," said Mama. Lydia sighed with relief. She would not have to stand over the hot tallow and dip the strings.

"Come, Mary, let's find your dolly," she said, taking Mary out of Mama's arm.

Mama put a stool by the cauldron for Charlotte to stand upon.

"*Dinna fall,*" she said, and it was not a warning but rather a command. If Charlotte lost her balance, she might fall headlong into the pot of scalding hot tallow. She must not even so much as brush against the hot cauldron, or she would burn herself.

It was lovely, being old enough to help Mama with such a dangerous task.

Mama let Charlotte dip the first row of candles. Holding the candle rod as steady as she could, Charlotte lowered the wicks into the melted tallow. When she lifted them back out, they wore a thin, shiny coat of tallow. At first the tallow coats were wet and soft, but they dried quickly. Charlotte counted to ten like Mama had taught her, and then she dipped again.

The wicks came up with thicker coats. The hot wax was making the long wicks kink up, and after another dip they had to be straightened out or else Mama would wind up with crooked candles. Charlotte could not both hold the candle rod and straighten the wicks, so Mama was the one to gently pull on the long strings until the kinks went away. When they were straight and cool, Charlotte dipped another time.

Dip, cool, dip, cool. The patient part was waiting for the tallow to harden between dippings. The kitchen smelled like fried salt pork. It was a hot and choking smell that did not make Charlotte hungry as real salt pork would have done.

"Bayberry candles are nicer," she announced.

Mama nodded, brushing a loose lock of hair out of her eyes with the back of her hand. Her face was pink all over and her eyes were red.

"We dinna have enough o' those to last

the winter," she said. "I didna get as many bayberries this year as I'd have liked."

Bayberries were picked in the autumn from the wild bushes that grew in the sandy places along the edges of the flats. One day every fall, Mama handed out pails to all the children, for the berrypicking. In the crisp salt-breeze air, with the warm sun shining down and the gulls wheeling over the marsh, Charlotte and Lydia and Tom and Lewis hurried to strip the small green berries off the bushes. They did not stop to eat any, for bayberries were not good to eat. But the person who filled a pail first got an apple turnover from Mama's basket, still faintly warm from the Dutch oven, oozing sticky, sweet juice through the corners of its flaky crust.

This year Tom had found the best bush and had filled his pail first. Then Charlotte and Lydia and Lewis worked all the faster, while Tom drove them crazy breaking off bits of crust and licking the rich apple filling that seeped through the cracks. Bayberry picking meant scratched fingers and shrieks of laughter and the soft *thup thup* of berries landing on other berries in the pail. And at last, full pails and turnovers all around.

At home the berries were poured into Mama's big black kettle and boiled until they dissolved into a thick, waxy, gray-green mass. This was bayberry tallow, and Mama dipped candles from it just as she did from animal fat. The bayberries gave off a fragrance like pine needles and spice. One bayberry candle could perfume a whole room. Mama saved them for company and Sundays. Tallow was good enough for ordinary nights.

Charlotte dipped the wicks into the tallow again, and Mama said the candles were fat enough. They were carrot shaped, thick as Papa's thumb at their rounded bottom ends and tapering to the width of Charlotte's little finger near the top of the string.

Charlotte held the rod still a few minutes longer, watching the cloudy yellow-white candles gently swing. She mustn't let them swing so much that they knocked into each other. The wet shiny wax grew dull as it cooled.

Then Mama took the rod and hung it in the lean-to where the air was cold and dry. The drying candles were like a row of icicles dripping from the ceiling.

All that morning, while Lydia played house with Mary under the kitchen table, Charlotte and Mama dipped candles. Their eyes smarted from the smoke, and their faces stung. Charlotte thought longingly of the cold, feathery snow outside; she would have liked to throw herself into a snowbank as she had thrown herself into the hay at Mr. Heath's husking. It would be cool and soft and glittering, like a bed of moonlight.

But she supposed she was so hot that she would melt the snow, and then her moonlight bed would turn into a puddle.

"Mama," she asked, "why doesn't snow ever stay *snow*? Why does it melt, or else it freezes and then it's ice?"

A little laugh escaped Mama. "Och, Lottie," she said, "you'd have to ask the good Lord Himself, as He's the one that made the rules. It's one o' the mysteries o' nature, I suppose."

But Mama saw Charlotte's frown and she paused a moment, her hand stilling the long-handled spoon that had been stirring the last of the melted tallow in the iron kettle. Her eyes smiled softly at Charlotte.

She said slowly, "But I suppose, after all, it's a mystery we spend a lot o' time rubbin' elbows with. Nothing stays the same, Charlotte, not snow nor water nor man nor beast. Think o' a seed, a pumpkin seed mayhap, that you plant in the garden. It doesna stay a seed, does it? There's somethin' inside it burstin' to get out, and it goes from a little hard flat pebble to a dainty green spike peepin' up from the ground. Then the spike turns to a nice fat stalk, and it puts out leaves. Then the blossoms come, and the pumpkins. And even the pumpkins when they're full grown are changin' every day, growin' riper, and then too ripe, and then, if ever a pumpkin was left to itself instead of being turned into someone's dinner, it would turn soft and rotten, and at last it would rot away into earth.

"It's the same with everything else in the world, Lottie. Babies are hardly the same for two days in a row, and wee girls turn to big girls while their mothers' backs are turned. Mountains wear down, rivers change courses, and nations expand their borders. Ice melts into water, and water boils away into steam. I canna think o' a blessed thing in all creation that stays the same forever."

From her nook under the table Mary squealed and grabbed for the battered corn-husk doll Lydia was waving in front of her. It was the doll Lydia had made at Mr. Heath's husking. Now it was ragged and torn, its arms crumbled off, its skirts crushed by loving baby fists. Still, Mary shrieked for it, scrambling to grab it as Lydia pulled it away. Lydia scooted backward, and Mary crawled out from under the table. She pulled herself to her feet and attempted to climb right over a chair in her efforts to reach the doll.

Charlotte could remember when Mary had been too little to walk. She remembered when the doll had been quiet leaves enclosing an ear of corn. She looked at the tallow candles dangling from their rod and remembered when they were just grease in Mama's frying pan. She was old enough now to remember lots of things, so that the mystery was not what things had been but what they would become.

The Tree in the Parlor

Sometimes in the December afternoons, neighbors came calling. Ladies came with their sewing or their knitting, to sit by Mama's parlor fire and keep each other company as they did their handwork. Mama loved to have visitors. She kept a tin full of ginger cookies in the cabinet, so that she might always have something to offer a guest, and she served her special hot spiced cider. Every day after dinner, she checked to make sure she had a little cheesecloth pouch of cinnamon bark and nutmeg ready to pop into a kettle of cider. To Charlotte, the sweet, rich, spicy smell of the hot cider was the smell of winter, even more so than the piney scent of bayberry candles or the crisp smell of snow in the air.

If the ladies had little boys or girls, they brought them along. Charlotte was expected to play nicely with them and to be a good hostess. She must let them play with her clothespin doll if they wanted to, and show them the buttons in the button collection she had decided to start. She had only three buttons in her collection so far: a plain wooden one with two holes, a smooth brown one made of carved deer horn, with four holes, and a shining brass button with no holes at all. Instead of top holes it had two very short legs underneath, with holes in them for the thread to go through. Will had given her this button before he went away. When she rubbed it with her thumb it gleamed so brightly that she could see her face in it.

Her friend Susan had begun a button

collection also. Sometimes Susan's mother came calling, with Susan's baby brother bundled up in layers and layers of blankets. Those were the best days, for Susan was Charlotte's very nicest friend. Charlotte and Susan would sit on the hooked rug in the parlor and play with their buttons and their dolls. Charlotte had Emmeline, in her cheerful blue-plaid dress, and Susan had amassed a whole family of corn-husk dolls. They made believe the buttons were the dolls' dishes, and Mama let them have little crumbs of cookie to put upon the plates.

Sometimes Mama went calling herself, and she took Charlotte and Mary with her. There was a Mrs. Edsel across Washington Street, in a little crowded house at the foot of Great Hill, who had seven yellow-haired children, and all of them younger than Lydia. Mama was fond of Mrs. Edsel, who spoke with a German accent as thick as Mama's own Scottish one, and who called Mama "Martha" instead of "Mrs. Tucker" and insisted that Mama call her "Wilhelmina" in return.

Charlotte loved the Edsel house, because it was so unlike other houses she knew. There was always something to look at that she had never seen before. On one visit in late December, Charlotte was surprised to walk into Mrs. Edsel's parlor and find a fir tree in a large pot on a little low table in the parlor. The tree was hung all around with decorations—strings laced with popped corn, and other strings threaded through round slices of dried apple, and walnuts that had been painted gold, and paper-thin sugar cookies cut into the most beautiful shapes: hearts, tulips, doves with tiny currant eyes. Charlotte's breath caught in her throat, while she stared at that wonderful tree.

Mrs. Edsel said it was called a Christmas tree.

"Tomorrow will come Christmas," she told Charlotte, "and we will put candles on the tree, ja, and in the windows, too, to make a light for the Christ Child."

"Really and truly?" cried Charlotte. She had never heard anything so wonderful.

Her family had a lovely party every New Year's Eve, which Mama and Papa called "Hogmanay" in the Scottish tradition. But they did not celebrate Christmas.

She asked Mama why *they* never had a Christmas tree.

"I never heard of it before, Lottie. Is it a custom from your old home, Wilhelmina?"

"Ja, from Pennsylvania. And before that, from Germany, where I grew up." Mrs. Edsel looked at her tree with proud and happy eyes. "Here in New England, not many people keep Christmas. Where we lived in Pennsylvania, it is a more special day even than the Thanksgiving Day."

Charlotte felt she could have stood there all day, breathing the good smell of that tree. The sugar-cookie doves looked at her with their bright little eyes. The white popcorn was bright and fluffy as clouds against the piney branches.

"I beg you please to excuse the state of mine house," Mrs. Edsel said apologetically, smoothing out her rumpled apron. "Today,

71

it is our busy day. I kept *die Kindern* home from school. We are all of us in a flurry, getting ready."

Mama's eyes skimmed over the table littered with cookie crumbs, coils of string, and snips of paper. The Edsel children stood around the table, their cheeks flushed red, their eyes dancing with excitement. The oldest girl, Hannah, was cutting away at a piece of folded paper while the second-oldest girl looked on critically. A heap of evergreen boughs lay half toppled on the floor beneath a window, and a dizzying array of good smells was drifting out from the kitchen.

"I beg your pardon, Wilhelmina," said Mama. "I see we've caught you at an inconvenient time. We'll not stay—I was only after droppin' off that weavin' draft you wanted."

"Ach, do not mention it, you need not leave," insisted Mrs. Edsel. "I will get you a cup of tea—"

But Mama shook her head and told her not to worry a bit. "You get on with your preparations. The tree is lovely; I've never seen such a sight."

At Mrs. Edsel's urging, Mama promised to come back the day after tomorrow—the day after Christmas.

"We will have many cookies and nice things left over—too many! You must come and help us eat them. You will like that, ja, Charlotte?"

Charlotte said she certainly would. She hated to leave. The Edsel children called out a chorus of cheery good-byes. They were too busy to play with Charlotte that day. Hannah Edsel was just laying down her scissors and unfolding the piece of snipped paper. Charlotte looked backward over her shoulder as Mama led her out the door, and before it closed she saw the paper open into a many-pointed star.

All the next day, as she helped Mama scour the parlor floor with sand, Charlotte was thinking of that star and the tree and the wonderful cookies. She wished she could have brought one of those cookie doves home to show Tom and Lydia. She wished she could wrap one up and send it to Will! How pleased he would be; he liked birds so much.

She said so to Mama, and Mama said he would indeed. But she said a cookie bird would never survive a trip to Maine, even if they knew just where to send it.

"Will would find a nice mess o' crumbs, I fear, and nothin' more!"

"We must make him some, then, when he comes back," said Charlotte firmly, "if Mrs. Edsel will give you the recipe. Do you think she will?"

Mama thought she would.

The day after that, the Edsel children were waiting for Charlotte at their window. They came running outside to greet her, and they pointed at the paper stars they had hung upon the bushes and the gate. They led her inside to show her how beautiful the house was with all its decorations in place. The evergreen boughs had been hung above the windows with bows of red ribbon, and more boughs were strewn upon the windowsill with tall bayberry candles rising among them. The candles were not lit now, because it was daytime.

Mrs. Edsel brought out a platter heaped high with cookies—not just doves and hearts and flowers, but other shapes, too—stars and hands and even little men and women! The men wore tailcoats, and the women had long full skirts. Their tiny cookie hands were raised as if in greeting. Charlotte could not bear to eat them; she held her little lady-cookie carefully in the flat of her hand.

But the Edsel children were calling to her.

"Hurry and eat, Charlotte; come and play with us!"

Mrs. Edsel's children knew a great many games. There were so many children in the family that there were always plenty of people to a side in any game that required the choosing up of sides, like Spanish Knights or Three Kings. They were lining up now for Here Comes a Duke, the boys on one side of the parlor and the girls on the other.

"Come, Charlotte!"

Charlotte left her cookie on the table and

ran to join the girls, while Mama and Mrs. Edsel sat beside the fire, talking, sipping tea, and keeping Mary and the Edsel baby from eating up all the cookies.

The two Edsel boys, Johann and Friedrich, stood on the side of the room facing the long row of girls. Besides Charlotte and Hannah, there were Marta, Elsie, and Bertha. Johann and Friedrich galloped up to them, singing:

"Here come two dukes a-roving,
Roving, roving,
Here come two dukes a-roving,
With the ransy, tansy, tea!
With the ransy, tansy, tario!
With the ransy, tansy, tea!"

They stopped before Hannah and sang out:

"Pretty fair maid, will you come out,
Will you come out, will you come out,
To join us in our dancing?"

Hannah tossed her head scornfully and

shouted, "No!" Everyone laughed, and the boys danced backward. They sang:

> *"Naughty girl, she won't come out,*
>   *She won't come out, she won't come out,*
>   *To join us in our dancing."*

Then they went to the next girl in line and sang the whole thing over again to her. That was Marta, and she answered, "Yes!"

So her brothers took her hands and the three of them danced in a circle. They sang:

> *"Now we've got the flowers of May,*
>   *The flowers of May, the flowers of May,*
>   *To join us in our dancing!"*

Then it all began again with the next girl in the row. Charlotte waited eagerly for her turn. She could not decide whether to say yes or not. It was such fun to whirl around the circle for the mayflower verse. But it was delightful, too, to toss your head and refuse the invitation with all the scorn you could muster.

"No!" she cried when they asked her. Her voice made the mothers jump a little, and all the children laughed.

But the next time the boys came down the row, Charlotte said yes and danced with them. They sang about the flowers of May, while all the time the pine smell of the Edsels' Christmas was thick in the air around them.

What the Bells Said

They began after breakfast, one morning in February. Mama had just gone out to fill the water pail, and Charlotte was in the frigid lean-to trying to keep Mary from running outside without a coat or hood, when the first faint peals came singing across the flats. It was only one bell, just at first. *Tong-tong, tong-tong.* Charlotte hardly noticed it. She was too busy shivering and trying to drag Mary back into the warmth of the kitchen.

But then a second bell joined in, wildly,

clanga-clanga-clanga-clang, as if the bell-ringer were doing a dance on the end of the rope. Charlotte forgot the cold. She ran to the door and looked out. Mama stood by the well, staring across the fields that separated the Tucker house from the Roxbury flats. Boston was on the other side of the flats, and the bells were church bells ringing in the steeples of Boston.

Another bell joined the clamor, and another. There was no separating the tones now; there was a cacaphony of bell song, growing fuller and louder, as if all the church bells in Boston were adding their voices to the glad outcry.

"Mama, what is it?" Charlotte called. Her breath made fog in the brittle air. "Why are they ringing?"

Sometimes, on Sundays, she heard a faint tolling from Boston, if the First Church of Roxbury bell did not drown out the sound. And if the wind was right, a silvery chiming could be heard every day just before dinner: the Catholic church in Boston, Mama said, reminding its parishioners to say their noontime prayers. But these bells were not *Hush! Time to pray* bells. Nor could they, at a little past eight on a Monday morning, be calling their congregations to worship.

Slowly Mama put down the water pail. "I've no idea," she murmured. Then, turning to Charlotte with a sudden light in her eyes, she told Charlotte to mind Mary for a moment while she went to see Papa.

"Get her into the house before the both o' you catch your deaths!" she called, her cloak flying out behind her as she hurried across the road.

"Mama!" Mary cried. The bells continued to peal. Though Charlotte's nose stung from the cold, she did not want to close the door against the gaily crying bells. But Mama had said she must take Mary inside. Reluctantly, she pushed the door shut and dragged Mary into the kitchen.

She could not hear the bells inside. She could scarcely have heard a bell if it had been ringing in the next room, for Mary was screaming with rage at having been prevented from following Mama.

But there were many more bells to hear that day. Not long after Mama had returned, her eyes sparking impatiently because Papa didn't know either what the bell-ringing was about, another clanging outcry arose. This time it was louder; it clanged right through the walls and made Charlotte jump. This bell's voice was an old friend; it was the First Church of Roxbury bell.

Mama snatched her cloak back down off its hook and once more told Charlotte to see that Mary didn't get into mischief while she was gone. Then she glanced at the fire and seemed to think better of it, for she said, "Never mind, you shall both come with me. Get your hood," and that was how Charlotte came to hear the grand news before her older brothers and sister did.

Already there was a crowd of men and women in the smithy, at Mr. Waitt's mill across the street, and in the street hurrying toward the common. Papa came out of the smithy when he saw Mama in the doorway, pushing through the crowd to stand beside her. Together they walked a little way down the road. The church bell cried out over their heads, and all around Charlotte, feet were crunching on the frozen snow. The sun glinting off the snow was like light frozen in ice.

"Peace!" a man called. "Peace! They've signed a treaty!"

Charlotte knew what *peace* meant. It meant the opposite of war; it meant the war was over.

It meant Will would soon be home.

She had been too little to remember the day the war began. But she knew she would never in all her life forget the day it ended. Never before had she seen grown-up people act the way they acted when the news rang into Roxbury. Big men were crying, and ladies that Charlotte had only seen sitting hushed and prim in church were cheering like boys at a bonfire. In the smithy, on the street, everywhere, people were clutching at each other's arms and asking questions. They all asked the same questions, and no one had answers.

Then a young man, panting, cried out that he had run all the way from Boston where the whole town was afire with the news of a peace treaty. Mama swooped Mary onto her hip and caught Charlotte by the hand. She moved them through the crowd until they were near the young man. Papa was a strong, quiet presence behind Charlotte, his sooty hand warm on her shoulder.

"An express messenger arrived from New York just before eight o' clock," the young man was saying. He climbed up on a rail fence at the roadside so that he stood above the crowd. "He must have come right through Roxbury, but he was under orders not to stop until he made Boston town. Rode like a madman, too—made the trip in thirty-two hours! He carried a letter from a Mr. Jonathan Goodhue of New York to the editor of the *Centinel*, informing that gentleman—"

Here the young man paused, breathing hard. The men and women of the crowd shifted their feet impatiently, and someone cried out, "Informing him what, man? Out with it!"

The young man grinned. Charlotte could just see his face over the shoulder of Mr. Waitt, who stood in front of her. She felt squeezed between the tall bodies all around her. But she clung close to Mama's side; she would rather be squeezed than go away and not hear what the young man was saying. The church bell was so loud that the young man had to shout.

"—Informing that gentleman of the arrival of a ship in New York Harbor—a ship bearing a messenger from Britain who had in his possession—"

"A treaty of peace!" Mama cried out.

The young man grinned again and nodded.

Huzzah! The crowd erupted in a cheer. Mama turned and kissed Papa, and Papa squeezed Mama and Mary with one arm and Charlotte with the other.

"Thank God, thank God," Mama was whispering. Charlotte saw that she was crying. Then Charlotte understood that the church bells were ringing out a thank-you to heaven, too. She was glad deep inside herself that the war was over.

The master dismissed school early that day. The big boys and girls came running home, shouting about the news. Lewis was whooping so loudly that Charlotte heard him coming even before he turned onto Tide Mill Lane. When he burst into the kitchen, with puffing Tom and rosy-cheeked Lydia on his heels, he was singing "The Star-Spangled Banner" at the top of his lungs. He had lost his hat somewhere; his ears were as red as his hair. When Mama pressed him about the hat, he admitted he had thrown it into the air a time or two and then must have forgotten to collect it.

Mama shook her head in exasperation. But no one could be angry for long on such a glad day.

After supper that night, Mama told Charlotte not to put on her nightgown.

"Put your Sunday frock on over the one you're wearing," Mama said, "and come back downstairs."

Charlotte had never before been told to do

such a curious thing. She hurried to pull her good woolen dress over her head; her arms felt thick and stiff in two layers of clothing, with her flannel underwear beneath. Down in the kitchen, Mama wrapped her up in a long red scarf so that only her eyes and the tip of her nose were left to peep out. Then she added Charlotte's hood, her cloak, and her warm woolen mittens. When Charlotte asked where she was going, her tongue tasted wool. Mama only smiled and looked wise.

"You shall see" is all she would say.

Lewis and Tom and Lydia were bundled up also. Papa wore his heavy coat and his new hat pulled low to cover the tops of his ears. He took Charlotte's hand, and they all went out of the house. Only Mama and Mary stayed behind in the warm kitchen.

The terrible cold cut immediately through all the layers of Charlotte's clothes. She remembered the last time she had been out at night, going to the husking in the autumn. She had thought it was cold *then*, but this— this was real cold. The stars were like bits of ice in the black sky. Her breath clung wetly to the woolen folds of scarf over her mouth.

"Are we going to church, Papa?" Tom asked.

"Aye and nay," said Papa cryptically. He strode past the smithy, which was quiet now, deserted, and turned onto Washington Street. Lydia complained that she was frozen and she wanted to go home. Lewis snorted and told her she was such a baby, she *ought* to be home in bed.

"Hush," Papa said.

Candles flickered in the windows of the gristmill. Charlotte saw silhoutted figures inside: tall Mr. Waitt, the miller, and some other men, with cider tankards in their hands and an air of excitement about them that was clear even when glimpsed through a window. As Papa led the way along Washington Street, Charlotte saw that many of the houses—most of them, in fact—had candles shining like beacons in the windows. When she looked down the street she saw a row of lights on either side, as if some of the stars had fallen out of the sky and landed on the roadsides.

"Is it the candles, Papa?" she asked. "Is that what we've come to see?"

"Aye and nay," said Papa again. She could not see his eyes twinkling in the dark, but she could hear the twinkle in his voice.

They came around the curve of the road to the common. Charlotte drew in her breath and her eyes opened wide. All around the common the buildings were blazing. Fire licked at every window. It burned inside the church and the town hall and the shops. It leaped in the windows of the big splendid houses along Dudley Street, which flanked the common on its south side. A great crowd of people milled around in the street outside the burning houses.

For a moment, Charlotte's heart did not work. Then she saw that the buildings were not burning down; they were only lit from the inside by candles and lamps. Every window had a flame dancing on the sill. Candlelight poured from the windows of the church, like rays streaming down from the sun.

"Oh," Charlotte breathed.

Lewis murmured, "By Jiminy!"

Papa said it was called an Illumination.

"In honor of the peace treaty," he said.

"Won't the houses catch fire, Papa?" Lydia asked, worried. Papa shook his head. He said the folks inside the buildings were watching the candles closely.

"You can see where they've taken down their curtains," he said, pointing at the wide windows of the Dudley Street mansions.

"How can there be anyone left inside?" Charlotte asked wonderingly, for the crowd milling about on the common was bigger than the one that had gathered outside the smithy that morning. It was as great a crowd as the one that had formed to see the militia off last fall—and that had been more people together at once than Charlotte had ever seen in her life.

It was too cold, Papa said, to stay outside for long. He did not let Lewis and Tom join the boys who were running about on the frosty grass of the common.

"Your mother will have my hide if I bring one o' ye home wi' frostbite," he said. "We'll just have us a good long look at the Illumination. It's a sight I'm not thinkin' you're likely to see too many times in your lives. Look hard, Lottie," he said, drawing Charlotte close beside him. "You must soak it all in so ye can tell it for your mother, when we get back."

Charlotte did not need to be told to look hard. She could not take her eyes away. She had never seen anything as beautiful as these golden, shining windows all around the dark and noisy square. The glowing lights seemed to dance just as the bells had sung that morning, as if bells and lights alike heard music playing, a hidden music that people could not hear.

Washington's Birthday

The next day some of the bells were
still being rung. Every hour a bell
called out from Jamaica Plain, one of
the little towns west of Roxbury. Now and then
a deep *boom* would startle the air, a cannon
being fired in celebration, and everywhere
flocks of birds would flap up from the trees.

Everyone, everywhere, was celebrating, it
seemed. Even the people who had been
against the war all along were celebrating.

The day after that there was more
celebrating than ever. That day would have

been a celebration day even if the war hadn't ended, for it was the anniversary of General Washington's birthday. General Washington was a great hero. He had helped America to win her *first* war against England, the War for Independence that had been fought even before Mama was born. He had been elected the first president of the United States. Washington City was named after him. So was Washington Street, right here in Roxbury. Mama said there was hardly a soul in the country who did not grow misty eyed at the thought of all that General George Washington had done for the brave new nation. Every year the whole country celebrated his birthday, to honor him. Washington's Birthday was nearly as grand a day as Independence Day, only without the fireworks.

This year, because of the war ending, there *were* going to be fireworks. This year, Papa said, there would be festivities the like of which none of them had ever seen.

"Us lads in the trades have got a wee somethin' up our sleeves," Papa said. His eyes sparkled with secrets. He wouldn't give even a tiny hint; he only smiled and said, "Ye shall see."

All morning Charlotte and Lydia and Tom danced with impatience. Papa and Lewis disappeared to the smithy right after breakfast, and Mama would not let the others go and see what they were up to. Tom was furious.

"It's not fair! Lewis ought to have to stay home, too, if I can't go."

Mama raised her eyebrows.

"Well, that's very generous of you, Tom," she said wryly.

Then Tom hung his head and frowned at the floor, for he knew he had been selfish. But Charlotte understood just how he felt. It *wasn't* fair, being left out of secrets just because you were younger. She and Tom would always be younger; Lewis and Lydia would always be ahead of them.

When Papa and Lewis came in for dinner, they could not help grinning at each other across the table. Their trousers were streaked with soot and there were bits of sawdust clinging to their shirts. Lewis had a splinter in his finger, which he kept picking at, furrowing his brow over it importantly, until Mama said he would cause it to fester and had better leave it alone.

"You're building something," Tom guessed. "What is it? What is it?"

But Papa and Lewis wouldn't say.

They gulped down their beans and sopped up the bean gravy from their plates with slices of Mama's good bread. Charlotte felt too tormented by curiosity to eat. She poked at her beans with her fork, hardly aware she was doing it.

"Eat up, Lottie," Mama scolded. "Or you'll miss the—" Her eyes flicked over toward Papa, and she folded her lips together. She wouldn't say *what* Charlotte would miss. Charlotte and Tom and Lydia looked at each other, and they all bent their heads over their plates and ate with furious concentration. Whatever it was, they were determined not to miss it.

Papa and Lewis excused themselves from

the table and left the house. Mama hurried Charlotte and Lydia through the washing of the dishes, and she sent Tom upstairs to change into his Sunday clothes.

Sunday clothes—on a Wednesday! The mystery seemed too great to be borne. Charlotte could not stand still when Mama buttoned her into her own Sunday dress. Papa and Lewis came back to the house and put on fresh clothes also, but they did not wear their fine Sunday shirts and trousers. Lewis had put on a red-and-white-checked shirt and plain brown pantaloons. Papa wore his spare set of work breeches and a clean shirt of homespun linen. They looked as though they were simply heading off to the smithy the morning after washday. Yet there was Mama rustling and lovely in her one silk gown, and Charlotte and Lydia with their best ribbons in their hair, and Tom scowling above his Sunday collar. Even little Mary was bedecked in her finest, her round cheeks glowing pink as rose petals above the snowy frills of her Sunday frock.

"We'd best be goin'," Mama said briskly. She nodded at Papa and Lewis. "You lads mustna be late."

"Late for what?" Charlotte pleaded.

Mama only said, "Lewis, stop sucking that finger. Shall I go after the splinter wi' me needle?" Her eyes went to the clock, and she frowned.

"No, ma'am!" Lewis said hastily. "We'll be late! It's fine, Ma, just a little speck."

Mama sighed. "Well, if it doesna work itself out by this evenin', I'm havin' a go at it."

Lewis shoved his hand into his pocket and hurried to the lean-to, snatching his coat off the kitchen peg on the way. Charlotte didn't blame him. She had been plagued by splinters herself, from running her hand along a wood rail fence, and once Mama had had to dig out the splinter with a sewing needle. Charlotte had screamed from the pain, and Mama herself had had tears in her eyes.

Papa followed Lewis outside. Mama said they were going on ahead.

"We'll meet up wi' them later," she said,

snuggling Mary into her little fur hood. "And you needn't bother askin' where they're goin'," she said lightly, interrupting Charlotte before she had gotten one word of her question out. "Curiosity killed the cat, you know."

Then Mama looked around at all of them: Tom's disgruntled frown; Lydia's anxiously wringing hands; Charlotte, who could not seem to stand still no matter how she tried. Her very toes were tingling to know what on earth was going on. Mama grinned a funny lopsided grin and said, "Aye, and many's the time it nearly killed me, as well. Come, my bairns, let's get to the secret before the secret gets you."

Bundled up, coats brushed, they all went out of the house. A dull gray sheet of cloud was pulled across the sky. The wind came sharply off the flooded flats, where gulls wheeled above the water. Their rough voices squawked impatiently, as if by scolding they could make the tide go out faster.

The smithy doors were closed again—

Charlotte could not remember ever having seen them closed in the daytime, except on Sunday. Papa and Lewis were nowhere to be seen. There were two long curving stripes in the soft dirt between the blacksmith shop and the road, as if something had been dragged across the ground. There was a patchwork of hoofprints in the dirt, although Papa had not shod any horses that day.

Mama hurried them past the shop and turned onto the main road. Washington Street was crowded again. Women in best bonnets and men in well-brushed hats nodded at Mama and smiled at the children. All of them were headed toward the common.

The two roads that flanked the common—Washington Street on one side and Dudley Street on the other—were lined with people. The common itself swarmed with laughing men and smiling women, and children running and hooting among them. There would not be room for a single sheep to graze, if ever a sheep had been stouthearted enough to brave the noisy, milling throng.

"We'll stop here," Mama said, leading the children onto the frosty grass at the edge of the road. She craned her neck down Washington Street, looking for something. She wouldn't say what it was, no matter how much Charlotte and Tom pleaded.

"It'll not be long now" was all she would say, smiling a knowing smile.

Waiting would have been agony, had there not been so much to look at right there in the common. The people everywhere were smiling and gaily chattering. Everyone was happy on Washington's Birthday.

Some men nearby were drinking cider out of a glazed clay jug. Each time one of them a took drink, he first raised the jug to the sky and made a toast.

"To General George Washington, finest man whoever lived!"

"Excepting present company, of course," joked another man. He caught Charlotte watching him and tipped her a wink.

They passed the jug around, each of them toasting the great man who had led America to victory in the Revolution almost forty years ago. Then they made a round of toasts to the heroes of the current war.

"To General Scott, champion of Lundy's Lane!"

"To all our boys who fell at Bladensburg!"

"To General Jackson, for giving 'em what for down there in New Orleans! We'd still be at war if 'tweren't for him!"

"What are you talking about, Horace?" interrupted one of the men, an elderly, bald-headed fellow who had wiped a tear from his eye when the "boys of Bladensburg" were mentioned. "Jackson didn't win the war. The treaty was being signed over in Europe about the same time them British ships hit the New Orleans harbor. Ole Jackson made a good job of it, whooping them the way he did—I ain't saying he don't deserve a toast; he's one of the best soldiers this country has got. But you can't go around saying he won the war, son. The war was already over when the fighting at New Orleans started!"

Charlotte was listening eagerly. Now that

the war was safely over, she liked to hear about the battles.

Another man, fierce eyed and younger than the others, took the jug from Horace's hand and held it up.

"To President Madison," he said, "for finally having the gumption to get us out of the sorry mess he got us into."

"Ah, Jack, let's not spoil the fun with politics," said one of the others. The man named Jack shrugged and took another swig from the cider jug.

"All right, then, how's this? To our own brave Roxbury boys, for having the courage to join the fight—and the sense not to do it until the fighting was near about over!"

The other men laughed, and the old man shook his head ruefully. He chuckled and reached for the jug.

"No arguing with that. It's our own fault, and we ought all of us to be ashamed of our foot-dragging. We should have passed that vote to send our militia two years ago, not just last autumn."

"Now who's getting political?" asked Jack. The group burst into laughter again. Then Mama nudged Charlotte and whispered that it wasn't polite to eavesdrop on other folks' conversations.

Charlotte sighed, for she hadn't meant to eavesdrop. Who could help hearing what was being said right beside you?

Suddenly a hush came over the crowd, and a faint noise rose above it. *Rat-tat-tat, a-rat-tat-tat.* And *dee-dee-deedle-dee*, high and sweet like the whistle of a bird. Everyone turned to look down the common, toward the point where Washington Street curved north on its way across the flats to Boston.

"It's a fife!" Lydia remarked.

"And drums," said Tom.

Charlotte's heart swelled up. "Mama!" she cried. "Are the soldiers coming home?" They had left on a day like this, with all the town on hand to see them off.

Mama shook her head. "Nay, love, it'll be weeks yet."

"Anyhow, they wouldn't be coming from

that direction," Tom put in helpfully. "Unless they came by boat to Boston, and Papa says they won't do that."

A cheer rose from the crowd. "Hurrah!" Children ran out into the road to see what was coming along it, and their mothers commanded them to come back.

Charlotte stood on tiptoe, straining to see.

"Perhaps I could help your little one, ma'am?" a gruffly polite voice asked Mama. It was one of the cider-drinking men, the older one who had corrected the man called Horace when he toasted General Jackson. He was gesturing toward Charlotte. Mama looked at him intently a moment, and then she smiled and nodded.

"You're very kind," she said. "Charlotte, how would you like a better view?"

"Yes, please," said Charlotte. She felt shy, but she wanted very badly to see what was coming. The drums and fifes were louder now, closer, and the crowd huzzahed and whistled all along Washington Street.

The old man passed his cider jug to one of

his friends, and he lifted Charlotte up in his arms. She could see heads and hats now, instead of trouser legs and skirts. She could see the crowd massed along both sides of the road, and someone marching down the road, a man on horseback, wearing a tall hat, with two other men on his right and left. The two marching men carried flags and waved to the crowd. Behind them came a wagon—a whole train of wagons—all of them filled with men.

"Who are they?" she cried. "Is it a parade?"

The old man chuckled and nodded his gray head.

"Your first, missie?"

"Yes, sir. No, sir. I'm not sure," said Charlotte. She thought she had seen an Independence Day parade once, but she could not remember for certain whether she had been there or only heard about it from her brothers and sister.

The old man laughed again. "I know just what you mean. Every parade is like the very first one."

"A parade, a parade!" Tom was shouting. He

whooped a whoop that was worthy of Lewis.

"Where are Lewis and Papa?" Charlotte worried. "They'll miss the parade!"

"They won't miss it," Mama promised.

But the parade was upon them. The man on horseback—Mama said he was the head marshal—waved at them as he passed. He wore a uniform full of gleaming brass buttons. The banner bearers grinned and waved.

"Hoorah!" shouted the crowd.

"Oo-wah!" cried Mary, clapping her hands.

Mama's laugh rippled out, because Mary had learned another new word.

After the marshal came the first wagonload of men. They stood holding on to the sides of the wagon, all of them swathed in shining white aprons. They waved bread-peels and rolling pins above their heads, and some of them were pitching small, round objects at the crowd.

"White-flour rolls," the old man told Charlotte. "Those men are bakers. Hoo-wee, I'd like to catch me one of them rolls."

"I'll get one, just you watch," boasted the

man called Jack. When the bakers' wagon passed, he leaped into the air, hands out-stretched. But his fists closed on air. Then Charlotte heard his friends burst out guffawing, for there stood Mama, triumphant, with Mary in one arm and a flour-dusted roll in her other hand.

The old man holding Charlotte quaked with laughter, and Charlotte and Tom and Lydia cheered. Some ladies nearby eyed Mama doubtfully and shook their bonneted heads. Mama paid them no mind. Mary was squealing and grabbing at the roll. Mama tore it into pieces and handed them around so that everybody got a bite of the soft, light bread—Charlotte, Tom, Lydia, Mary, the kind old man, and even abashed Jack.

But there was no time for Jack's friends to properly tease him, for the next wagon was passing, pulled by four patient horses. This one conveyed a sight so astonishing Charlotte could not speak. There in the back of the wagon, a group of leather-aproned men were constructing a small brick building!

Four low brick walls rose from the wagon bed. The walls were growing higher every minute, for the men were slapping on mortar with their trowels and setting new bricks in place.

"Mortar here!" cried one bricklayer, and a boy—the apprentice, Charlotte guessed—hurried over with a bucket and trowel. The crowd applauded wildly as the masons went past.

"What's going on, Mama?" cried Lydia, perplexed. She had seen many parades before, but none like this.

"It's a mechanics' parade," Mama explained. "All the men from the different trades about town have put together displays to show the work that they do."

Her eyes sparkled, and suddenly Charlotte gasped. The full meaning of Mama's words struck her all at once. Papa was a mechanic—blacksmithing was one of the trades, too, just like bricklaying and baking.

"Is Papa—?" she cried.

Mama beamed.

"My papa's in the parade!" Charlotte told the kindly old man who held her. "And my brother Lewis!"

"Aw, shucks!" cried Tom in a voice that was half excited and half dismayed. Charlotte knew at once that he wished he was in the parade, too.

"Hush, Tom," said Mama. "Look, here come the hatmakers."

Charlotte clapped and cheered at the sight of gruff Mr. Stock standing solemnly in the back of a third wagon, wearing not one but three hats stacked each on top of the other upon his head. The crowd screamed with laughter. Other men, who made hats in shops in neighboring towns, stood alongside him wearing samples of their trade, too. One man even wore an enormous, beribboned, flower-decked lady's bonnet.

"It suits you, Cleveland," called out one of the bystanders.

The man named Cleveland grinned and dropped a mock curtsey in thanks. Charlotte and Tom and Lydia were laughing so hard their bellies ached. Charlotte waved to Mr. Stock, and he looked right at her and with grave courtesy tipped each of his three hats to her, one by one.

More wagons rolled past, each one funnier or more impressive than the last. The house-wrights had constructed a miniature building, painted white, complete with slender columns and with candles shining in the windows. A sign waved above it; Mama said it read "Temple of Peace." Charlotte could hardly believe such a lovely little building had been put together in a day, just for the parade.

The printers were rolling sheets of paper off their printing presses and sailing the inky sheets out to the crowd. Someone nearby caught one of the sheets and read from it a poem that he said was titled, "Song of Peace." But the crowd was too loud for Charlotte to catch many of the words. She could not have listened properly, anyway. She was too excited, waiting for Papa's wagon.

The tinsmith had a wagon—there was Sam

Dudley, grinning at the crowd—and the coopers, with men busily making wooden barrels as they passed, and the block makers and stone layers and truckmen.

And at last there came a wagon pulled by a pair of familiar oxen. They were Mr. Heath's oxen, and it was his wagon. He sat on the wagon seat, driving. Behind him, in the flat bed of the wagon box, were Papa and Lewis, splendid in their leather aprons, with their sleeves rolled up above their elbows despite the chill of the February day.

Charlotte's mouth fell open. In the back of Mr. Heath's wagon Papa had constructed a small forge. Real coals shimmered red from a cast-iron drum, and Lewis was pumping air into them with a handheld bellows. Papa's anvil was mounted on a block of wood beside the forge, and as he rolled past, Charlotte saw him lift a piece of red-hot iron from the glowing coals. He held it up, calmly inspecting it. After placing it upon the anvil he began to hammer and shape it—for all the world as if he were standing on solid ground in his own

smithy instead of in the back of a moving, pitching wagon! Before the eyes of the crowd he transformed the iron rod into a perfect, beautifully shaped fireplace poker.

Charlotte's heart swelled with pride. Her papa, her brother, up there for all the town to see. She cheered wildly, Tom whistled and shouted, and Mama utterly forgot herself and leaped up and down, bouncing Mary, calling out, "Hurrah for Lewis Tucker, finest smith on either side o' the Atlantic!"

The cider-drinking men howled with laughter, and the crowd cheered and clapped. Even Papa could not help himself; from his perch in the wagon he met Mama's eye, and his mouth quirked to the side. His shoulders shook with silent laughter. Lewis beamed proudly at Charlotte and Tom and Lydia above his bellows.

Charlotte yelled louder than she had ever yelled in her life, hurrahing for Papa and Lewis. No one scolded her; all around her everyone else was cheering, too.

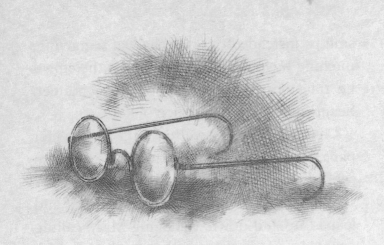

Infection

Lewis's finger did not get better. Mama took out the splinter with her needle, but it did not seem to help. At breakfast time a few days after the parade, the finger was red to the knuckle, with pink streaks running down the finger toward his wrist. When Mama looked at it, her forehead creased into lines. Lewis pulled his hand away with a shrug that meant, "It's nothing." But Charlotte saw how he tried to hide the hand in his pocket and then pulled it right back out as if the pocket had teeth.

Papa examined the finger, and his eyes looked like Mama's forehead.

"Infected," he said, and Mama snatched her bonnet off its peg.

"I'm calling in the doctor," she said. Her voice was hard and angry. Then Charlotte began to feel afraid, because Mama got angry at the things that frightened her. She saw that Lewis's finger frightened Mama.

"Martha, sit down and eat," Papa said. "I'll go."

"I said I'll go and I'm goin'," snapped Mama. Her sharp voice made them all flinch. Charlotte and Lydia and Tom looked at each other with furtive darting glances. Charlotte felt as though she had been splashed with cold water. But Papa's quiet eyes regarded Mama gently. He did not seem to mind having been spoken to so harshly. He said nothing, but his eyes were telling Mama things.

Mama's cheeks flushed red and her fingers yanked at the bonnet strings. "Dinna you fret, Lew," she said, and Charlotte wasn't sure whether she was talking to Lewis or to Papa.

"It'll be fine. Happen it looks bad and feels worse, but it's all in a day's work for Dr. Prentiss."

Her cloak swirled around her shoulders and she was gone out the lean-to door. Charlotte and the rest of them sat staring at the food that had grown cold on their plates. The whole house seemed colder, with Mama gone.

"What's the matter with all of you?" demanded Lewis irritably. "It's not as though I'm dying or anything. It's only a stupid finger."

But his voice had a tremble in it. He shot Papa a pleading sort of gaze. Papa smiled at him and said, "That's right. Lydia, pass the potatoes, there's a lass."

The parlor was heavy with the sounds of forks clinking on plates, mugs thunking on the table, mouths chewing and chewing. The fire crackled cheerfully as if it, at least, was unconcerned by little red lines on a finger. Mary, tied onto her long-legged, high-backed stool beside Mama's empty seat, fussed and would not accept the pieces of fried potato Lydia tried to feed her.

"Ma, Ma," she called, craning her head around toward the kitchen. She smacked a bit of potato out of Lydia's fingers, and it flew across the table, hitting Lewis on the head. He put up his hand to brush the potato out of his hair, and then he winced and pulled the hand away, cradling it in his other palm. When he caught Papa watching him, he flinched away from the gaze as if somehow it hurt him as much as the finger did.

Charlotte watched in confusion. She thought about how Papa had said "infected," in the same dull tone with which he might have said "war." She wanted to ask what it meant, but something in Lewis's eyes made her afraid to. Why should a little splinter cause so much worry? She'd had plenty of splinters herself in the past. Mama pulled them out or sometimes picked them out with a needle. They hadn't made red streaks under the skin. No one had gone running for a doctor.

Papa's plate was empty, but he did not get up and go to the smithy. Lydia scolded Charlotte to finish her breakfast and told Tom, who was eating potatoes right off the platter in the middle of the table, not to eat like a pig. Tom stuck out his tongue at her. It was covered with potato. Lydia shrieked, and Charlotte laughed. Her voice was too loud. Lydia stared daggers at her, as though Charlotte had done something dreadful, like laughing in church. Lewis stood abruptly and went out to the kitchen. She heard him easing on his coat and striding out of the house.

Papa seemed to come back from thoughts that had taken him a long way away. "Shouldna be out in the cold, wi' that fever," he muttered, and he too went for his coat.

The lean-to door closed behind him. Charlotte and Lydia and Tom looked at each other.

"He has a fever?" asked Charlotte.

"From the infection," said Tom.

Lydia got up and untied Mary from the

high chair. "Here, bairnie, let's clean you up," she said as if she were Mama, wiping Mary's hands and face with a napkin. Tom went around to Lewis's plate and began quietly eating the cold and untouched potatoes there.

"What's infection?" Charlotte asked them. "A very bad splinter?"

"No . . ." said Lydia pensively, while Mary screeched and shrank away from Lydia's scrubbing napkin. "I think . . . it's when there's poison in your blood. Like when Mr. Heath's spotted cow scratched herself on that nail, and pus came out. Remember? She wouldn't get up, and her eyes looked like yellow glass."

"But that's different," argued Charlotte. "That was a cow."

"It's not different," Lydia insisted. "I bet the poison got into Lewis's blood through the splinter hole, just like it got into the cow through that scratch."

Charlotte shook her head, not understanding. "But I've had lots of—"

"It doesn't happen *every* time," put in Tom,

in a superior voice that would have made Charlotte mad if she hadn't been so desperate to know more.

"They'll have to cut off his finger," Tom added, taking the last bite of Lewis's breakfast.

Charlotte gasped and turned to him in horror.

"They *will*?"

"Or else he'll die."

Lydia burst out shouting. "You just shut your mouth!" Her voice was so fierce that Mary began to cry. Charlotte saw that Lydia was afraid. She felt afraid, too, now, and she almost hated Tom for being able to say such horrible things.

Tom shrugged stubbornly, not meeting anyone's eyes, and muttered, "The spotted cow died, didn't she?"

"Stop it!" cried Lydia. "You don't even care! Lewis could die, and you'd just be glad there'd be more food for you to eat, you fat old *pig*!"

Charlotte couldn't help it; tears were spilling out from inside her. There was a part of her that wanted to scream like Mary. Tom's face crumpled, and he stared at Lydia in disbelief, as if she had punched him in the stomach.

"I would too care," he said in a tiny, choked voice.

Lydia looked uncomfortably at the floor. All the rage seemed to drain out of her at once.

"I know," she said.

"Maaaaa!" wailed Mary, and at the same moment Charlotte heard the front door open and close.

"I'm right here, love," said a surprised voice, and Mama came into the parlor in a rush of wind and woolen cloak. Her clothes carried a frosty out-in-the-cold smell, but Mama was warm and crackling as fire. Her sparking eyes took in the untidy table, the red eyes, the howling baby.

"Where's Lewis? And your father?" Her voice was not sharp as it had been when she left. It rose smooth and calm over Mary's cries. Charlotte ran to her and buried her face in Mama's skirts.

"Will he die, Mama?" she sobbed. "Is Lewis going to die?"

Lydia was sobbing, too, and Tom's eyes leaked.

"Ma!" shouted Mary, suddenly ceasing to cry. Her small hand whacked Lydia on the back, and her baby eyebrows were drawn together in a stern and reprimanding glare. It was as though she had got fed up with all the fussing and was scolding them for ignoring her.

Despite their worry, all of them laughed. Tom's laugh was husky with tears that had been wanting to come out. Mama took Mary out of Lydia's arms and cuddled the baby on her hip.

"Saucy miss. We dinna like it when the world stops revolvin' around us for one minute, do we?" Mary patted Mama's cheek happily. Charlotte's heart swelled with hope and relief.

"It'll be all right, then?" she asked. "The doctor will fix Lewis's finger, right?"

But Mama's eyes, though calm now, were shadowed.

"We must pray that he shall, Lottie," she said softly. "He's coming right behind me. I told him I'd not stay while he got his coat on. There he is now—Charlotte, get the door." Mama became a whirlwind of activity, clearing the table, issuing commands, wiping noses.

"Tom, go and find Lewis. I expect he's in the barn. Send him in, and fetch your father, too. The young fool—" Charlotte knew she did not mean Papa; she meant Lewis, for going out in the cold when he had a fever. "Charlotte, take Mary, and for pity's sake keep her quiet. Give her a lump of sugar from the bowl—only one, mind—and find her something to play with. Give her your button box. Let me take your coat, doctor. My lad's hidden himself in the barn, I fear. He's afraid you're going to take the finger."

Her voice faltered, and she fairly snatched the doctor's coat and hat out of his hands. Dr. Prentiss bobbed his head understandingly. He had a long red face and round gold-rimmed spectacles. Charlotte saw that his side-whiskers were unevenly trimmed; the left one was a little longer than the right one. He wore a high white collar with a bunched-up scarf, orange as a pumpkin, tucked into the front of it. It was such a high collar that Charlotte wondered how he could move his head at all.

He must have felt her staring at him, for he looked her way and gave her a kindly nod. When he nodded, his chin disappeared into the pumpkin-colored folds of the scarf.

Then Papa and Tom came into the kitchen, followed by a sullen, ghastly-looking Lewis. Lewis's cheeks burned red against a pale, waxy face. Mama hustled the younger children into the kitchen and made them stay there alone while the doctor examined Lewis's finger in the clear light of the parlor window.

Charlotte and Tom and Lydia were too frightened to talk. They watched Mary suck happily on her lump of sugar, and after a while Lydia took the cone of hard-packed sugar back out of the sideboard where she had put it away, and she broke off a lump for each of them.

Silently they sat licking their sugar lumps, listening for noises from the parlor.

The End of the Road

The doctor stayed a long time. The children heard grown-up voices talking, talking, and after a while a husky, choked kind of sobbing that scared them worse than had the sight of the angry red finger. It was Lewis, crying. Charlotte had never heard her big brother cry before. She could scarcely recall ever hearing *Tom* cry, much less Lewis.

The days after that were strange, almost dreamlike. Nothing went according to its usual way. No bread was baked on baking day. Neighbors came calling not just in the afternoons, but in the morning, at chore time, any time at all. It didn't matter; Mama wasn't doing any chores. Papa did all the barn work, and Lydia fed the chickens.

The neighbor ladies brought food so Mama wouldn't have to cook. Mrs. Waitt brought a crock of beans, and Mrs. Edsel delivered two whole loaves of rye-and-Indian bread. The loaves were still warm from the baking. Mrs. Edsel would not come into the house; she said she didn't wish to intrude. She only handed her basket of bread to Lydia and said to give Mama her regards.

"Tell to your mother that I will be glad to help in any way I can," she said kindly, her blue eyes filled with concern. Charlotte winced away from the pity in those kind eyes.

The mystery of how a little wood splinter could make a person so sick was to Charlotte a greater mystery than all the other questions she had ever had. Though the splinter was long gone, it had allowed the sickness to get into Lewis's blood. The sickness was a fever, and not even Mama, with all her knowledge of herbs and cures, could make it go away. It got worse instead of better.

"Dinna you fret yourselves; Lewis will be fine," Mama said brightly. But it was a prayer, not a promise.

Papa moved Will's bed downstairs into the parlor. It was a small bed, just big enough for one person. Mama emptied the old crushed straw out of Will's mattress and filled it up again with goose feathers from her own big feather tick. Afterward, Papa and Mama's mattress was flat, half full. Mama said it would do, for now.

Charlotte didn't like that phrase—*for now.* It left open a door for frightening thoughts about what would happen then.

But Mama would not permit anyone to indulge in frightening thoughts.

"He'll be right as rain," she said, over and over. "The fever will break soon."

The parlor was the sickroom, now. Lewis lay in the new feather bed beneath a heap of quilts and blankets. Often, in his sleep, he kicked them off, and then he would wake, shivering, teeth chattering, and beg for fire and covers. Sometimes his voice sounded like crying, like a little boy younger than Charlotte.

It was the fever that made him cry like that.

The doctor had made a tourniquet for Lewis's finger. He wrapped the finger tightly with a thin strip of cotton cloth. He took a short stick, a bit of twig, and twisted it around the cloth in a special way. Now the stick made a kind of handle, and every day the doctor came to turn the handle a little more. That made the string twist a little tighter around Lewis's finger.

The red, swollen finger turned purple, then black. It gave off a bad smell. It was dying. One day, Mama said, it would simply fall off.

"And Lewis will get well?" Charlotte pleaded.

Mama nodded forcefully. "Aye, he will."

"But his finger won't ever grow back?"

"Nay, lassie. He must give up the finger to stop the infection from spreading. He's a brave lad, a fighter."

But the pity grew stronger in the neighbor ladies' eyes. They kept asking Mama if they couldn't "take the others off your hands for a spell, Martha, dear." These invitations brought Charlotte's heart into her throat every time. She didn't want to go away and stay in someone else's house.

To her great relief, Mama refused the offers politely, every time. She said Lewis ought to have his family around him. She kept Lydia home from school to help look after the baby. Poor Tom had to go off alone in the mornings, the dinner pail dragging his mittened hand toward the ground as if it contained stones instead of bread and cheese.

All that long week, the fever lived in the Tucker house. Mama hardly left Lewis's side for a minute, except to go into the lean-to and break off bits of the dried, crumbly herbs that hung from the rafters. She brewed these into teas that she dripped into Lewis's mouth with a spoon. Her herbs could not cure him, but they could ease his pain, she said, and make him sleep more deeply.

"Rest is his best medicine right now," she said.

She wouldn't rest a minute, herself. Papa grew stern with her at dinnertime and made her sit down in the kitchen for a few bites. The family was eating all its meals in the kitchen now, at the old scarred table there where Mama chopped her potatoes and kneaded her bread. That was another thing not right. Every small piece of the day was uncomfortably altered. Mrs. Waitt's beans didn't taste like Mama's. No one remembered to tie back Charlotte's hair with a ribbon, and it fell forward onto her plate while she ate. There was no lively chatter at meals, as there had always been. It was quiet, except for the sounds of Lewis moaning in his sleep, in the parlor.

Sometimes he cried out in a clear, strident voice, as if he were talking to someone.

"Put it down, Tom! It's a snake, put it down!" he would call, though Tom wasn't even in the house; he was at school. Or: "Who put the cookies in the fire?" and then, worse than the crying, Lewis would laugh a high-pitched giggle that brought goose bumps to Charlotte's arms.

Papa said he was having fever dreams. When Lewis called out like that, Mama would drop her fork and hurry into the parlor, to cool Lewis's searing forehead with a damp cloth and to murmur to him in her soothing voice.

After meals, Lydia and Charlotte cleared the table and washed the dishes. They did it without being asked. Papa smiled at them on his way out the door to the smithy. He must keep on working, even with Lewis so sick. There was more work than ever for Papa to do, for he had no one to help him.

All the rest of the day, when they weren't eating or clearing up, Charlotte and Lydia entertained Mary and listened to the sounds of the parlor. Mama had drawn her spinning wheel close to Lewis's bed; as she spun, she sang to him: sad, low Scottish songs that did not march and dance as Mama's songs usually did.

The End of the Road

"Ye banks and braes o' Bonnie Doon,
How can ye bloom sae fresh and fair?
How can ye chant, ye little birds,
And I sae weary, full o' care?

"Ye'll break my heart, ye warbling birds,
That wanton through the flow'ry thorn,
Ye mind me o' departed joys,
Departed never to return."

The spinning wheel hummed mournfully, and Lewis moaned in his sleep.

At last Charlotte felt she could not bear it another moment, and she ran into the parlor.

"Sing something else, Mama, please!" she cried, even as Mama was starting to her feet, her angry look rushing to her face.

Mama opened her mouth and then froze, staring at Charlotte, and something soft came into her eyes. She put a finger to her lips and pointed at Lewis on the bed. His hair was damp and matted, and he turned his head back and forth on the pillow. Mama held out her arms for Charlotte. Silently Charlotte went to her and buried her face in Mama's apron. Mama's strong arms were around her.

Mama hugged her a long time, and then she smoothed Charlotte's hair and gestured for her to go back to the kitchen. She didn't speak.

After that, Mama did not sing the sorrowful songs anymore. She did not sing any songs at all. There was only quiet and rustling in the parlor, and Lewis's groans.

That evening the doctor came again. He was in the parlor with Mama and Papa for a long time; then he came into the kitchen for hot water, and his face was very grave. He didn't look at Charlotte or the others, sitting at the cluttered table with their suppers grown cold on their plates—even Tom's supper. He dipped water out of the black kettle that always hung over the fire and poured it into a dish, and then he returned to the parlor. No one came out to tell the children what to do. The fire in the kitchen hearth burned low, and lower. Outside, the cold darkness beat at the windows. Mary cried for Mama and then got sleepy in Lydia's arms. After a long time, Lydia said they might as well clear up and get ready for bed, so they did.

Tom lit a candle so they would have light to undress by. He wasn't allowed to carry lit candles, but Mary was asleep and Lydia couldn't carry both the candle and the baby. They crept into the hall and tiptoed up the stairs to their bedrooms. With each step they were listening to the parlor. The doctor's low voice rumbled through the board walls, but Charlotte couldn't tell what he was saying. Mama and Papa were so silent she half wondered if they were still there.

At the top of the stairs, Tom said he could change clothes without the candle. The moon was tipping a little light through his window, outlining the dark shapes of the bed and closet. Tom muttered a good night, solemn and owlish, and went into his room. Charlotte held the candlestick with two hands and followed the glowing circle to her bedroom.

In their room, Lydia and Charlotte put on their nightclothes, said their prayers with all their might, and blew out the candle. They tucked themselves into bed, with Mary between them. They left her in her daytime dress, for changing her would wake her up. Lydia said Mama wouldn't mind.

"We'll make believe it's a nightgown," she whispered to Charlotte. That was enough for Lydia; she could pretend things so well that they became real.

But Charlotte could not turn Mary's blue woolen dress into a white linen nightgown, no matter how hard she tried. She lay in the dark, feeling the blueness of the dress next to her, and the woolliness, and the jam stain down its front. All the time she was listening for Mama's voice or Papa's or Lewis's. She felt as though she had done nothing but listen since the day Lewis's finger turned red. Even with Mary and Lydia next to her, it was lonely in the dark with nothing to hear.

Then it wasn't dark any longer, and there was something to hear. Mama was singing, down in the parlor.

The End of the Road

"Every road through life is a long, long road,
Filled with joys and sorrows too,
As ye journey on how your heart will yearn
For the things most dear to you.

"So keep right on to the end o' the road,
Keep right on to the end.
Tho' the way be long, let your heart be
strong,
Keep right on round the bend."

Charlotte was wide awake in an instant. That was a song that had marching in it, and dancing.

She rushed downstairs in her nightgown and bare feet. Mama's voice was coming from the kitchen, and Charlotte burst in, her feet skittering over the sand on the floor.

"Mama!"

It came out a shout, but really it was a question. Mama knew, and she smiled at Charlotte.

"Hush," she scolded, though her singing had

been just as loud. "Your brother is sleeping. He's resting well, now. The fever has broken, thank the Lord." Her eyes were shining. "Lewis will be just fine."

This time it *was* a promise.

Mama said the worst was over now. The infection had passed, and the poor finger would soon be gone.

"It's a mercy it was only his little finger. He'll get along well enough without it. He'll not be the first smith to lose a finger; and Lord knows it could have been worse."

A delicious sizzling smell of salt pork was filling up the kitchen. Mama let Charlotte help her make biscuits, to go with the pork. Charlotte measured the flour, three cups, and the baking powder, one teaspoon. While Mama whirled her wooden spoon around the mixing bowl, her song kept stealing back out of her mouth, because she was happy and because she was in the habit of singing while she worked. Charlotte felt as though her heart was singing, too.

The End of the Road

"With a big stout heart to a long steep hill,
We may get there with a smile.
With a good kind thought and an end in
view,
We may cut short many a mile.

"Though you're tired and weary, still
journey on,
Till ye come to your happy abode,
Where all the love ye've been dreaming of
Will be there at the end o' the road."

Sharp Tongues

The first day Lewis was allowed out of bed, Mama roasted a turkey for dinner. She bought a fat gobbler from the turkey drover and stuffed it with bread and sausage and some crumbled sage leaves from her store in the lean-to. She roasted it in the tin kitchen. That was a large, three-sided tin box that sat on the hearthstones before the kitchen fire, with the turkey hung on a spit inside the box. Every now and then Mama turned the spit, so that a new side of the turkey would face the fire.

A pan fit into the bottom of the spit to catch the drippings, and the drippings would become the gravy for the stuffing.

Everyone kept saying how good that turkey smelled. Lewis sat on a chair in the kitchen, pale and weak but quietly triumphant, for he had cajoled Mama into letting him out of bed a full day before the doctor had said he might get up. He said he felt fine now. Charlotte did not see how he could feel fine, with his poor finger dying beneath the bandages and the tourniquet wrapped tightly around it. But Lewis shrugged and acted as if losing a finger was no worse than clipping one's nails. He said he expected he'd be back at work in the smithy in no time, and he said it in an iron tone that dared anyone to disagree.

He wouldn't let anyone look at his finger, or talk about it. When Mama had to change the bandage or adjust the tourniquet, Lewis ordered all the other children out of the room. Charlotte and Tom and Lydia felt half crazy with curiosity to know what the finger looked like beneath the cotton rags that Mama had tied around it. Was it purple-red and oozing, or black and shriveled? Would it just fall off one day, or would it crumble away like the burned wick of a candle?

Lewis wouldn't tell them, and he would not let them see. He told them to mind their business. Mama said if they couldn't give their brother some peace, they'd have to stay out of the kitchen. No one wanted to do that. They had been kept apart from Lewis for so many days, they couldn't get close enough now.

Lydia and Tom fretted so much about having to go to school that Mama had said they might have a holiday on the day Lewis got out of bed. So there was a crowd in the kitchen that morning, with the fat turkey hissing and popping on the hearth and Charlotte and the others clustered around Lewis's chair.

Charlotte felt almost shy with Lewis. She wanted to squeeze next to him on the chair, but she was afraid of getting too close to his bad hand. Lydia was holding Mary, standing beside Lewis's chair, and Mary kept grabbing at Lewis's hair. She did not do it because she had been worried about him; she grabbed because she liked to seize hair whenever she could get it.

Tom was sitting on a stool between Lewis and the fire, idly drawing on his school slate with a well-chewed slate pencil.

"See," he said now, showing the slate to Lewis. "It's Mr. Stock, from the parade."

Lewis's laugh was almost his old boisterous bellow.

"That's grand, Tom. With his three hats and all. Only, old Stock has bushier eyebrows."

"You mean *Mister* Stock, young man," corrected Mama, but her voice was tender. She was enveloped in a cloud of steam, draining the water out of a pot of boiled potatoes. She saved the water in a jar for making bread with later.

Tom's own eyebrows were huddled together in concentration as he worked at improving his portrait of the gruff hatmaker. Charlotte leaned on Lewis's knee and peered over the top of the slate at an upside-down Mr. Stock above the three splendid hats. She felt so happy that she did not mind in the least when Lewis complained that her elbows were boring holes in his leg.

She remembered how Mr. Stock had tipped each of his hats to her, one, two, three. How Papa had hit the hot iron with perfect blows of his hammer, despite the moving wagon. How tall and fine Lewis had looked, fanning the coals with his bellows.

The parade, the Illumination, the clanging news of peace: these things seemed a long time ago. Charlotte remembered now how her whole self had been filled up with the music and light of the celebration—and then it had been crowded out of her mind and she had not thought about it once in a week.

She realized with a sudden pang that she hadn't thought about Will either. She had been so glad to know he would soon be coming home, and then she had forgotten him.

She asked Mama if he would come home today. Today seemed like such a good day for coming home: the kitchen felt like Thanksgiving, with the turkey roasting and the drippings hissing in their pan, and a mountain of mashed squash waiting, fluffy and golden, in a crock on the hearth, and two pies crisping in the brick oven. It was a feast, and with Will home there would be twice as much to celebrate. Lewis better and the soldier returned!

But Mama shook her head and gave Charlotte a half smile. "It's hardly been two weeks, lass; the army's scarcely had time to pack up camp. Our boys willna be home for weeks yet. At any rate, you're after forgettin' that 'home' to Will isna here—it's his father's place in Dorchester. He'll be headed there first, I'm sure, and his mother'll want to keep him for a good long visit. His sweetheart, too! You remember Miss Keator, dinna you?"

Charlotte remembered. Her name was Lucy, and Will was going to marry her.

"Why does Will love her?" Lydia asked. "She isn't a bit pretty."

"Lydia!" cried Mama, stopping short in the middle of wringing a wet cloth over the dishpan. "For shame!"

"But it's *true*, Mama," protested Lydia. "Her skin is so rough, and—"

Mama's blazing eyes made her snap her mouth shut.

"The girl has pockmarks, yes, from the smallpox. She lost her whole family to the pox but for her father, and him an ailing old man. Lucy Keator is a good, kind lass with a clever mind and a stout heart. Our Will is a fortunate man to have a woman like Lucy at his side." She had resumed her squeezing of the dripping cloth, and now she gave it a final hard twist over the dishpan. Drops of water rained into the pan. "I'm surprised at you, Lydia, speakin' so cruelly."

Lydia's face was puzzled. "I didn't mean to be cruel, Mama. I was only saying what's true."

"Are you really such a fool as that, Lydia? Surely I've taught you better than to speak every unkind thought that comes into your head, just because you've thought it?"

Lydia's blue eyes were round and scared.

The rest of the children were frozen, listening. Tom's slate pencil was quiet in his fingers. Lewis was picking at his bandaged hand, scowling fiercely. Charlotte looked at him and saw that Lydia had made him as angry as she had made Mama.

Mama was very angry indeed. She shook out her dish towel with a crack and hung it to dry on the string that was stretched across the opening of the hearth, glaring at the towel as if it were a hateful thing.

"You ought to catch the smallpox yourself, Miss Lydia!" Lewis burst out. "I'd like to see *your* face all scarred over."

Lydia stared at him, aghast. She began to cry, her hands pressed to her face and her long fine hair pouring around them.

"That's enough!" cried Mama. "You ought to be ashamed of yourselves."

No one said anything for a moment. Mary did not like to see Lydia crying. She reached up her chubby hand and patted Lydia's bent head. At another time it might have been funny, but there was no smiling inside

Charlotte right now. She felt cold and hot all at once. She hardly dared to look at Mama. She looked at Tom instead. His eyes were very round.

At last, Mama let out her breath in a sigh. "Ah, me," she said. "I suppose it's as the Good Book says: Just as a great forest is set on fire by a tiny spark, so too is the tongue a fire. Do ye see what a blaze we've set off with our careless words? All our fun spoiled, because some of us—and that's includin' myself—let our tongues wag without benefit of kindness nor charity. I ought not to have called you a fool, Lydia. But I do hope that all my children will look deeper into a person than at the scars on her face."

"Aye, Mama," Lydia murmured. "I beg your pardon."

Charlotte waited for Mama to speak to Lewis about his cruel words, but Mama only gazed at him thoughtfully. Her eyes were very soft and kind.

"Did ever I tell ye," she said suddenly, "o' the time my mother tied a stick to my tongue?"

148

That was so interesting it dried up Lydia's tears. All of them, even Lewis, clamored for the story.

Mama took the door off the brick oven and peeked in at her pies.

"They want a few more minutes," she said, and she sat down behind the small spinning wheel she kept in the kitchen, for filling up the odd moments of time between other tasks. Her hand set the wheel spinning and her foot moved the treadle. She did not so much as glance at the linen as it turned from flax to yarn between her fingers.

"I was about eight years old," she began, "a bit older than Tom and a bit younger than Lydia. A saucy, impertinent thing I was, till it's a wonder my mother didna lock me in the attic until I learned to behave myself."

"Were you really so naughty as that, Mama?" Charlotte asked eagerly.

"Very nearly," said Mama frankly. "I was a wild lass, who'd rather drink fish oil than behave like a young lady. But dinna you go gettin' any ideas. I was blessed with a mother who was the sweetest, most patient woman that ever lived. *You* children are not half so fortunate, for 'tis no secret impatience is the fault I struggle with most. If one of my own bairns gave me half the worries I gave my mother, there'd be trouble, all right!"

Mama pretended to glare around at all of them sternly. Charlotte laughed. She could not imagine any other mother being nicer than her own.

"Well, I must have been in a particularly impertinent way at that time, for even my mother's patience was wearin' a bit thin. My sister Grisie and I couldna speak a word to each other without squabblin', and though I always felt Grisie was the one who started it and I a victim of injustice, I can see now that I must have plagued my sister sorely. I was ever pesterin' her or leaving smudges on her needlework or making fun of her suitors behind their backs. Och, ye can see that my sister had good reason to be vexed with me, and 'tis no wonder she snapped at me now and again. Then I'd get into a temper and call her names and gibe and taunt; and when once you fall into the habit of using your tongue to wound people, it's difficult to get out of it. I began to speak impertinently to everyone, not just my sister. My governness hardly knew what to do with me—and then one day I was rude to my own mother!

"Och, the surprise on her face! She couldna believe I would lash out at her like that. As soon as I'd spoken, I wished I could be takin' the words back. But it was too late. You never can get them back, once they've come out. My mother looked at me, and her eyes were terribly sad.

"'Oh, Martha,' she said, 'I'd rather you beat me with a stick than speak to me so cruelly. Indeed, you *have* given me a kind of beating, the very worst kind, for what you struck was my heart.'"

"I threw myself upon her and sobbed out how sorry I was. I was, too, sorrier than I'd ever been in my life. But Mum told me quietly that it wasn't enough merely to be sorry; I must work to break the cruel habit of hurtin' people with words. 'If you're going to use your tongue like a stick,' she said, 'then happen it belongs with other sticks.'

"And she sent me outside to find a twig, a short thick one, she said, about the same length as my tongue. Then she took a bit of thread and tied one end around the stick and the other around my tongue. Och, it was terrible, with that stick danglin' out of my mouth, pullin' on my tongue, and the string so strange and uncomfortable-feeling. I couldna speak at all without that stick bobbin' and pullin'. I had to go about that way for an hour, and I dinna ken what was worse—the discomfort of the stick pullin' on my tongue, or not being able to chatter away as I was used to! I learned my lesson well, I can tell you, for though I still sometimes speak a harsh word in anger, I have not once since that day deliberately said something to wound another person.

"And if I do it by mistake, I'm very sorry and I beg the person's pardon. Just as I begged your pardon, Lydia, for callin' you a fool. It was wrong of me, and I'm sorry."

Charlotte saw that Lewis's cheeks had grown very red. For a moment she feared his fever had returned.

Then he turned to Lydia and murmured, "I'm sorry. I didn't mean it, you know. About the smallpox."

"It's all right," said Lydia.

"Och, me pies!" cried Mama suddenly, springing up from her chair. She snatched up a towel and took off the oven door once more. The smell of baked apples came pouring into the room. The turkey drippings sizzled in their pan, and in the hearth the flames leaped cheerfully.

The Wedding Supper

In March, another letter came from Will. It was dated six weeks earlier, before the peace treaty had made its way from Europe to America. Will wrote of the bitter cold of the Maine coast and of seabirds swooping above a gray and restless sea. He said the soldiers had had little to do; the British ships patrolling the Portland harbor had made no move to attack. The men in his unit, he said, were beginning to grumble, wondering if they had been marched hundreds of miles to do nothing but sit, while their fingers froze and their rations dwindled.

Will himself did not grumble. He said he supposed there were folks in Portland sleeping easier at night, knowing the army was standing ready to defend them; and that, Will said, was reason enough to be there.

But I do confess to wishing for better grub. We have beans, beans, and naught else. I guess I have eaten more beans this winter than all you folks down in Roxbury put together. And mind you that's including young Tom.

As a matter of fact, there are nights I dream that I am slowly turning into a bean myself. A big one, long and skinny, like a pole bean. I fear one of these hungry fellows I am with will come along and pitch me into a pot.

Beside these words, he had drawn a picture of a large bean standing upright on spindly legs, with two waving arms and a smiling face. The bean had short bushy hair like Will's own. Lydia and Tom screamed with laughter when they saw it. Charlotte held the page close to her face and studied it. The bean's eyes were just like Will's.

It gave her a shivery feeling, as if Will might really come home looking so peculiar. She wanted him to come home just the same as he had been when he left.

Papa said by now the army would be well on its way home. The Roxbury men should come trooping into town sometime next month, he guessed, unless the muddy roads slowed them down.

The weather was still cold and there were patches of old snow on the ground. But in the thicket across the road from the house, buds were beginning to swell on the forsythia bushes. Charlotte and Tom played out there between the bare slender trunks of the birches. They found an empty nest where, last year, a towhee had sat upon her eggs. The nest was empty now; the little red-sided bird and her babies had all flown south for the winter.

Soon it would be spring, and the towhee might return to her nest. Charlotte checked it every day (although Tom said that was silly, since spring wasn't here yet). Would the towhee come back first, she wondered, or would Will? Everywhere around her the hushed, chilly world seemed to be waiting: waiting for spring and sun and the twittering voices of the birds and the soldiers' fifes.

One thing happened in March that was not at all a *waiting* kind of thing. Mama had been wrong last fall when she guessed that Miss Heath and Sam Dudley would be married by the end of the year. Their wedding did not take place until the end of March, when the yellow forsythia blossoms had burst open on the bushes and the daffodils were nodding all around. The Reverend Mr. Tubbs was to marry them, and the Tuckers were invited to the wedding supper.

Charlotte and Lydia wore new dresses made of store-bought fabric, a buttery yellow cotton printed with deep golden flowers. There were ruffles of white lace around the sleeves and the neck, and for each of them a wide satin sash. Charlotte's sash was leaf green, and Lydia's was cherry red. Even Mary had a satin ribbon—rosebud pink—to trim her little frock. She looked like a buttercup, all in yellow, with a rose-petal sash.

Those yellow dresses were the finest dresses the girls had ever worn. Mama said they could afford them, because the war was over. The harbor was open in Boston once more; the merchants were once again able to send their ships full of cargo to other cities on the American coast, and to lands across the sea. Good trade meant the merchants and the craftsmen had more money, and that meant they could afford to pay Papa to do all sorts of work for them. All the past month Papa had been busier in his shop than ever. Lewis helped him as much as he could, despite the bandages that were still on his hand. Papa's customers were paying him in coin, rather than in hay or grain or squash or rabbits. He had given Mama a stack of silver coins and told her to buy a new suit of clothes for everyone in the family, to wear to Miss Heath's wedding.

The Wedding Supper

Tom and Lewis had new matching jackets and trousers—Tom's suit was a vivid orange red color, which he hated, and Lewis's was a more sedate dark blue. Papa had insisted that Mama buy herself satin to make a new gown; she had not had clothing half as fine as she deserved in years, he said. Mama tossed her head and said she would be ashamed to mince around in expensive satin, when there were so many more important things the household needed, but Papa held firm. He threatened to go to Bacon's store and buy the satin himself, if Mama did not. Mama had shuddered, laughing at the thought of what kind of cloth Papa might come home with if he did the choosing, and so she had gone to Bacon's herself and bought a lovely shimmery satin in the deep green color she loved best.

She made it into a gown with tight sleeves, puffed at the shoulders, and a high sashed waist. Beneath her bosom the satin flowed in soft straight ripples to the floor. When Mama moved, light played upon the green folds like sunlight glimmering on leaves. Ringlets of her auburn hair glowed beneath a green satin bonnet. Charlotte could not get enough of looking at her. If Mary was a buttercup, then Mama was a linden tree with the sun caught atop its branches.

Papa's eyes shone at the sight of Mama in that dress. But she scoffed and said it was the foolishest expense she'd ever heard of.

"Me black silk would've suited just fine for a neighbor's weddin', Lew Tucker," she said, sighing, as she surveyed herself in the looking glass. "I've not worn frippery like this since—well, since you ken when."

There was a peculiar note in her voice, half laughing, half annoyed.

"When, Mama?" Charlotte asked, thinking there must be a story in Mama's mysterious words.

But Mama only shrugged her shoulders and said lightly, "Ah, there was a time when I had to wear a peacock's feathers, lass, and I didna like it a bit. Hen feathers are more fittin' for the likes o' me."

Papa's deep laugh rang out. "My Martha,

a common chicken? I think not. If ye're anything, ye're a hawk or a falcon—aye, a wild thing, sleek and swift."

"You're daft, Lew," said Mama, rolling her eyes.

But Lydia called out, "You're a falcon with the voice o' a thrush!"

Papa slapped his forehead. "Aye, that's so, I was forgettin' the song!" He grinned. "Ye're right, Martha, I was bein' daft. Ye're no falcon—ye're a skylark, of course. Soars high, nests on the ground, sings the happiest song in the heavens. I ought to have seen that right away."

"I've never in me life heard such nonsense," Mama scoffed. She smiled at Charlotte. "You'll notice he wound up pickin' a bird that's as plain and brown as a hen. So you see I was right all along about the foolishness of these fine feathers!"

Papa chuckled, and then he rose from his chair and looked down at his own new suit of clothes. His mouth twitched ruefully and he shifted his feet from side to side, like a restless horse. He said Mama had paid him back for his "foolishness" by making him dress like a fool. Instead of the old-fashioned knee breeches Papa had worn all his life, Mama had made him a pair of pantaloons, the long-legged, loose-fitting trousers that all the young men were wearing. Charlotte thought Papa did look strange in his new costume, but she liked it. He seemed even taller than usual, and he was stylish and dashing in his smooth brown jacket and tall hat.

There were over two dozen guests invited to Miss Heath's wedding supper. They stood in the Heaths' large front parlor and watched as the Reverend Mr. Tubbs married the glowing couple. Miss Heath's chestnut hair was coiled upon her head, with little fat sausage curls hanging down all around. Charlotte liked those sausage curls. They were smooth and neat and orderly, and they waggled from side to side when Miss Heath moved her head. Miss Heath's cheeks were very pink. Her gown was a soft dove gray. At her waist she held a cluster of daffodils tied with a pink satin ribbon.

Charlotte could not take her eyes off the bride. She could hardly remember last summer, when no-nonsense Miss Heath had held her pupils to strict order in the schoolhouse. With a start, Charlotte realized that Miss Heath would not be her teacher this summer. Married ladies did not teach school. There would be a new schoolmistress—or perhaps a schoolmaster. Perhaps he would be strict and harsh like Master Phelps.

Charlotte felt a sudden churning in her stomach. She didn't want a new teacher. She wanted things to be the same as they had been last year.

There was no time to think about it just then, for the Reverend Mr. Tubbs was saying, "man and wife," and Sam Dudley, who was rather red in the face, was leaning toward Miss Heath to kiss her.

Then Miss Heath was Miss Heath no longer. She was Mrs. Dudley now. Charlotte stared at her teacher, trying to see how she had changed. She did not look any different. She looked just as she had a moment ago, laughing and rosy, her eyes bright with joy.

Miss Heath—Mrs. Dudley, Charlotte had to keep correcting herself—guided the guests toward the long dining table, where a supper of roast beef and baked pudding had been laid out. There was a long, low table for the children, made of a door set flat upon some benches. Charlotte knew this because Tom lifted up the white linen tablecloth to see. There were no chairs; the children ate their supper standing up. Besides the Tucker children, there were Miss Heath's—Mrs. Dudley's—nephews and nieces, the children of her brother Abe and her older sister, Mrs. Zeloda Hutchison. Charlotte knew the Abe Heath children from school and church, but the Hutchisons lived clear on the other side of Roxbury and went to the Jamaica Plain school.

The grown-ups made a big noise of laughing and jesting at their table. Charlotte ate her roast beef slowly and listened to the grown-ups behind her. Mostly they talked about the war's end, how relieved they were and how times would be easier now that trade was opened back up.

"I hear Ezra Custer is moving his family back to Boston," someone said. "Now that he can get his ships back in the water."

"Aye, that's so," agreed Mama. "I'm glad for Mrs. Custer—it's been hard going for her this past year, uprooted from her home as she was, and her husband so worried about losing his business. Things will be quite all right for them now. But I fear it's a sad turn for my wee daughter, for she's grown that fond of little Susan Custer she'll be brokenhearted to lose her."

"Whisht, Martha," came Papa's quiet voice. "Wee pitchers have big ears."

Charlotte sat frozen with a lump of beef in her mouth. She had not known that Susan was moving away.

She could feel Mama's eyes upon her, but she did not turn around to look. She was afraid she might cry, right there in the middle of the wedding supper, and disgrace herself.

"Charlotte, what's wrong? Don't you like

your supper?" asked Lydia beside her.

"I'll finish it for you if you don't want it," said Tom.

Charlotte nodded and slid her plate toward her brother. She chewed and chewed and chewed the bite of roast beef in her mouth, but it would not go down. All through the rest of the meal she tried to swallow that one bite of meat. At last she spit it into her napkin and folded up the napkin so that no one would see.

She hoped that when Mrs. Heath washed her table linens, later, she would not know that Charlotte Tucker had been the one to leave a bite of chewed-up meat in her napkin.

She had been so excited to be invited to the wedding supper, but now she could not wait to go home. She wanted to climb into Mama's lap. She wanted Mama to tell her it was a mistake. Susan was not going to move away; Charlotte and Susan would sit beside each other in school this year just as they had done the year before. They would share their dinners and take care of each other's dolls.

Miss Heath would still be their teacher. She would teach them how to embroider this year; they would make alphabet samplers like they had seen the big girls make last summer.

But inside herself, she knew Mama could not tell her any of those things. What was true was true, and what wasn't, wasn't. Miss Heath-the-teacher had become Mrs. Dudley-the-wife, and Susan's father was going to take his family back to their home on the other side of South Boston Bay. Those truths were as stubbornly real as the mouthful of beef she had not been able to swallow.

Spring News

In May, two waves of travelers came to Roxbury.

First came the birds. The warblers and the swallows, the finches and thrushes— the woods were full of them, and the trees in the dooryard fairly quivered with song. Shorebirds came winging back to the flats: the long-legged herons, the wood-brown ducks, the graceful white swans. The towhee returned to her thicket, calling out once more in her cheerful way, "Drink-your-TEA! Drink-your-TEA!"

And then, at last, the soldiers came home. They drifted back in twos and threes, for the militia unit had been officially released from service. Sam Dudley's brother came home in time to help the neighbors raise a barn for the newlyweds. Joshua Frisbee, who had lost his rabbit to the eagle up in Maine, came home and asked his own girl to marry him just as soon as he could find a house. He'd had enough of trail life, he said, and he couldn't wait to sit beside his own hearth fire and whittle in a rocking chair.

"This war has made an old man of me," he told Papa.

He had dropped by the Tucker house in the evening of the very day he returned to town. Mama's eyes had lit up when she saw him, for they all knew that Joshua and Will were good friends, and if Joshua was back, that meant Will was close at hand.

"I suppose our Will went straight on to Dorchester?" Mama asked. "If I'm not mistaken, he'll be after askin' his own sweetheart to marry him, first thing."

But Joshua Frisbee pursed up his lips and looked at the floor. Charlotte saw that he could not look Mama in the eye. His own eyes were shadowed, sorrowful.

"I'm afraid not, ma'am," he said huskily. "That's what I've come to tell you. I knew you'd want to know right away. Will hasn't come back. He . . . he was wounded, missus. That's what I've got to tell you. The redcoats came ashore in a raid and swarmed us. I saw Will go down; he took a shot in the leg, a bad one."

The clock ticked loudly on the mantel. Charlotte looked from Joshua to Mama and then quickly away. She could not look at the fear in Mama's eyes. She heard the sound of Joshua's swallowing, and Papa clearing his throat.

Lydia broke the silence. "I don't understand," she said hesitantly. "I thought the war was over a long time ago."

"It was," said Joshua, "but we didn't know it, and neither did the redcoats. Takes so long for word to travel that the war'd been over for months before we ever heard about it. Them redcoats was breaking the treaty when they raided us, but they didn't know it and neither did we."

Lewis spoke abruptly. "Is Will dead?" he asked, and it was nearly a shout.

Joshua shifted in his chair.

"I . . . can't rightly say. He was alive when I left him. But it was a powerful bad wound, son, near about tore his leg in half. I hated to leave him, but the lieutenant gave the orders. Will's up there in a hospital camp outside of Portland . . . if he's still alive. The doc said there was some infection, and he'd most likely have to take the leg."

Lewis got up abruptly and went outside. Mama looked at Papa, and Papa murmured, "I'll go."

He nodded at Joshua and went quickly out the front door.

Joshua's hands were wringing his weather-stained cap. "I ought not to have spoken in front of the youngsters," he said in an anguished voice. "I'm awful sorry, Mrs. Tucker!"

"Dinna fret yourself," said Mama softly. "Happen it would have been better for us to break the news to the bairns ourselves. But what's done is done, and you canna have known. Our Lewis had a bit of a battle himself wi' blood poisonin' this winter. We came near to losin' him." She ran a hand over her face. "And now this."

All the rest of that week it seemed as if the birds were the only creatures making noise around the house on Tide Mill Lane. The sheep and the cows were not around to make noise, for they had been lct out to pasture. Mama did not sing; she hardly spoke. Lewis was darkly silent. He was staring all the time at his injured hand, rubbing the stump where his finger had been. The tourniquet and bandages had come off long ago, the poor finger was gone, and the wound had healed. Still, Lewis held the hand as if it hurt him, and he was angry if he caught anyone looking at it.

Charlotte wanted to look at it. She wanted to see it up close, how the new skin was stretched over the knuckle. She saw how well Lewis was able to get along without the lost finger, and that made her wonder if it would be as easy for Will to manage with only one leg.

She could not imagine him with only one leg. What would happen to the empty side of his pantaloons? Would they flap around behind him as he walked? How could he walk, with one leg missing?

Then she would remember that he might not have any legs at all anymore. He might be dead. *Dead*.

Lambs died, and chickens, and dogs. Sometimes other people's mothers or fathers died. She had heard of that, and she had heard of babies dying. She had even seen Mama crying once, and when she had asked Mama in a panic what was wrong, Mama had told her not to worry—she was only sad because a baby she knew had died. Charlotte had been afraid it was her friend Susan's baby brother, but Mama said it was not anyone Charlotte knew.

Lewis had almost died. The whole time he was sick, Charlotte had known he might die. But she had not been able to think beyond the *might die* to *dead*. She could not imagine a world without Lewis in it. If he had died, his death would have been a going-away. Will's death was a never-coming-back. He was gone already, and he would just go on being gone forever.

The thought made Charlotte feel cold and scared inside. She felt angry, too. They had all been so happy when Lewis got better, and now, as Mama said, *and now this*.

One day Mama said it was time to begin the spring cleaning. She said the best way for Lydia and Charlotte to help her was for them to keep Mary occupied, out of harm's way. The girls were glad to leave the house and go out into the bright, windy, springtime world. The lilac bush beside the house was just beginning to bloom; the sweet, heady smell was the smell of earth warming and eggs waiting in nests. The mountain laurels shook their pink-blossomed branches at the sky. The ground was muddy from the spring rains, and the mud sucked at Charlotte's shoes when she walked.

Lydia carried Mary past the garden and the barn, where the mud was worst, and set her down on the other side of the rail fence that ringed the sheep pasture. Lydia climbed over the fence, and then Charlotte did. Mama's sheep were all down at the far end of the pasture, their newly shorn backs looking pink and scrubbed. Mary laughed and pointed at them; she wanted to go and pet them. But the girls did not have to go anywhere—the sheep came to them, baaing and pushing against Lydia, to see if she had brought them anything nice in her apron pockets.

"Run and get some oats," Lydia instructed, and Charlotte clambered back over the fence and hurried to the barn. The wide doors stood open, sunlight slanting in and pushing back the shadows inside. High above in the rafters, great spiderwebs trembled in the breeze. The air was cool and dim and heavy. Charlotte used the milking stool to climb up to the oat bin, and she filled both her pockets full of the slippery grain.

She thought about going up to the loft to look for the barn owl's nest, and to play with the kittens that Papa said had been born up there last week. Their mother was a tiger-striped mouser who lived in the barn. She was a friendly cat; she liked to keep Mama company at milking time. But Papa had said all cats, even friendly ones, liked to keep to themselves when they had newborns to tend to. And Lydia was waiting. Charlotte went out of the barn, climbed up on the stone wall that ringed the garden, and balanced on its length until she reached the back pasture.

Tom was there now, too, scratching the lambs behind their soft ears. They butted their heads against him, nuzzling his hands and his shirt. Mary, held safely above the sheep on Lydia's hip, squealed and tried to pat all their heads at once. There were six ewes and four lambs. They had black faces and wide flat noses. Their soft ears drooped down toward the ground, and their plaintive baaaas were very loud.

"Did you bring something to eat?" Tom asked Charlotte hopefully.

"Oh, yes," said Charlotte, scooping the grain out of her pocket to show him. But he made a face and said that wasn't what he meant.

"I meant for *us;* I'm hungry!"

The sheep at least were happy. They crowded close around Charlotte and licked at her hand. Their wide blue tongues were rough and slimy all once. Mary reached frantically toward Charlotte, calling out, "Some! Some!"

That was one of her first real words, and Charlotte laughed to hear her say it. She poured a little grain into Mary's palm and laughed again to see the way Mary thrust it toward the sheep, spilling most of it.

"Some! Some!" she cried again.

Tom sighed and looked toward the house. "Do you think," he wondered aloud, "do you think Mama would give us some cookies?"

But none of them wanted to go back and ask her.

"You just had breakfast, Tom," scolded Lydia in a grown-uppish voice. Tom rolled his eyes and sighed again. He didn't like it when Lydia tried to act like Mama. Charlotte didn't either. Sisters should be sisters and leave the mothering to mothers. She wished people would do what they were supposed to, instead of jumbling things up.

"Breakfast was an hour ago," Tom grumbled. "I've been working up an appetite since then. Had to sweep out the whole smithy and fill up the water tub. Now I'm hungry all over again."

"You could eat wild onion," said Charlotte helpfully. She pointed at a clump of long, narrow green leaves spiking out of the ground amid the clover and the grass.

Now Tom made a face at Charlotte. "Onions don't fill up your belly. I wish Mama'd make doughnuts. She hasn't made doughnuts since I don't know when."

"She made them last week," Charlotte contradicted. She knew, for she had helped Mama twist the long strips of sweet dough before they went into the kettle of boiling fat. "You ate them all up."

"That's because you're a pig," said Lydia in her maddening motherly tone.

"I am not either!" Tom shouted, outraged. "Anyhow, I'd rather be a pig than a stupid goose. Pigs are smart."

Tears sprang to Lydia's eyes. She could not bear to be called stupid. Charlotte knew it was because she was afraid she really was stupid. She hated that she was last in her class at school.

"You're mean, Tom," Lydia muttered, sniffling. Mary turned away from the sheep and put her sticky hands on Lydia's face. She patted Lydia as she had patted the sheep.

Lydia cuddled Mary and kissed her. Glaring around the baby's head at Tom, she carried Mary a little way off into the field. Some of the sheep followed them, nudging Lydia's legs in hopes of more grain.

Charlotte fed the others the rest of the grain in her pocket. She stroked their soft ears. Their backs were stubbly where the new wool was growing in. Papa and Lewis had shorn them last week, the same day Mama had made the doughnuts.

That was also the day Joshua Frisbee had come to their house. Charlotte looked at Tom and suddenly she felt very cross with him. Too many things were not the way they ought to be. Lydia kept bossing; Tom was always nice and now he had been unkind; and Will was maybe dead—Charlotte did not want to think about that. Her insides ached from trying not to think about that.

"Why doesn't Papa go and get Will?" she asked suddenly. "Someone ought to go. Maybe he needs a nurse, like Mama nursed Lewis when he was sick."

Tom's round eyes blinked at her solemnly. "Papa can't go anywhere; he has too much work. If he leaves now he'll lose all his customers, and then we'll starve."

The worry was very strong in his eyes. He could not bear to think about starving any more than Charlotte could bear to think about Will being dead.

"Someone ought to go," she repeated stubbornly. "I'd go if I was big enough."

"Maybe his own mama and papa will go. They live in Dorchester, you know," Tom said.

"I know," said Charlotte impatiently. "Is that closer to Maine?"

Tom shrugged. "I don't think it's much closer. You can walk there in an hour."

"Oh," murmured Charlotte. "Well, maybe they'll go anyway. They could ride a horse." The idea took hold, and she began to feel better. "I bet they're already up there in Maine. I bet they're bringing Will home, and he'll have a bandage like Lewis had."

It was such a hopeful thought that she became quite convinced that was what was happening. Will and his parents were most likely already on their way back home, and Will would be bound to come back to Roxbury in a week or two.

She felt like running, so she galloped at the sheep, making them scatter. They ran away toward Lydia and Mary, their short tails bobbing behind them.

The New Teacher

Charlotte waited all spring into summer, but Will did not come. The tender green shoots of corn began to come up in the newly planted garden, and the early peas grew fat upon the vines. Rabbits ate all of Mama's lettuces, down to the last leaf. The hens began to lay again, and the cows each birthed a calf. Mama had milk to cook with, and cream, and good rich butter. Every day there was something new upon the dinner table: crisp watercress, salad greens, dandelion leaves. Mama grew nasturtiums along the garden fence, and picked the bright orange flowers to eat with fresh raw leaves of spinach.

School started. This summer, for the first time, Charlotte went alone. Tom had grown too old for the summer school, and besides, Papa needed his help in the shop. There was more work to be done than one smith could handle, Mama said, between the usual springtime rush and the new stream of customers passing through: the teamsters traveling through town with their wagons piled high. Ships were once more free to sail in and out of Boston Harbor, and that meant shiploads of cargo to be hauled in and out of Boston. Papa kept at his forge late into the night, these days, repairing wagon axles and harnesses, plowshares and harrows.

Even with his four-fingered hand, Lewis was a great help to Papa. He would be a fine smith someday, Papa said.

"Tommy, too," he always added, although Tom was too young to do more than fetch tools and sweep. "'Tis a fortunate man I am to have such good help."

This made Tom very proud, and he did not at all mind missing school.

Charlotte felt proud, too, because she was old enough to go to school by herself. She was not a bit frightened to make the walk alone. She knew the way, and besides, hadn't she once walked halfway to Boston all on her own?

On the first day of school, Mama kissed her good-bye and slipped Charlotte's dinner basket over her arm. Charlotte felt very big as she strode down the lane to Washington Street, the basket pulling on her arm. She was careful to hold it steady. If there were cookies inside, she was determined not to break them. It was tempting to peek beneath the green-striped napkin to see what Mama had put inside, but Charlotte thought it would be more grown-up to wait until dinnertime.

Then she saw Susan Custer on the road ahead of her, where Washington Street met Centre Street. Charlotte forgot about acting like a grown-up and raced toward her friend.

"You didn't move!" she cried. She had been

afraid Susan would leave without saying good-bye.

"We go next week," said Susan sadly. "My papa says it's silly for me to go to the Roxbury school for just one week, but my mother said I might as well. She has Auntie Hester to mind the baby."

"I'm glad. I don't want to sit with anyone but you," said Charlotte fervently. She held Susan's hand all the way to the schoolhouse, and they set their dinner baskets next to each other on the shelf in the entryway. They did not sit on last year's bench, for they were older now. They sat on the next bench over. The bench had no back, so that they could sit facing the window with a desk before them, or facing the center of the room, where the teacher's desk stood. The teacher's chair was empty, and all the talk in the schoolroom was about who the new teacher would be.

Half the pupils thought it would be Master Phelps, from the winter school, and half thought it would be someone new. One or two girls felt certain Miss Heath would come back this year, despite her being Mrs. Dudley now.

"I know she isn't coming," Charlotte said. "She called on my mother the other day, and she said she wasn't."

"Of course she's not! She has to keep house," put in one of the older girls. Her name was Freda Gregg. She was a big girl of eight years old, almost too old for a summer school.

"Pshaw!" scoffed Georgie Waitt, the miller's son. "I should think she could teach school and keep house both. Better than handing us over to that mean old Master Phelps."

"Hush, suppose he hears you!" cried Charlotte. "Suppose he's the one? He whips, you know."

"If he is the one, I'm *glad* I'm moving to Boston," Susan whispered in Charlotte's ear. Charlotte nodded miserably, feeling a sudden wish to move to Boston herself. She could not bear the thought of spending three months with strict Master Phelps, who would strike a pupil's hand with a pointer if she did not know her lesson correctly.

Just then steps sounded in the entryway, and they all knew the teacher was coming in. Charlotte and Susan squeezed hands tight. Was it a man's tread or a woman's?

Skirts rustled into the room, and all the students seemed to exhale at once. The new teacher was a woman, with smooth brown hair and a plain gray skirt.

She turned to face the class, smiling pleasantly. Charlotte's breath caught in her throat—she knew this person.

She was Will's Lucy!

Her face was very pale, and her blue eyes were sad. Here and there on her cheeks were the little dented pockmarks Lydia had spoken of so long ago. She was thin and plain, not a bit like pretty Miss Heath whom all the girls had so admired.

But her smile was warm and friendly. It was a crooked smile, drawn a little to one side, that made you feel as if she was about to let you in on a secret. Charlotte remembered how much she had liked this Lucy when she

met her last autumn, the day Will went away.

"Good morning, children," the teacher said. She introduced herself as Miss Keator and said she was looking forward to getting to know all of them.

"I see one or two familiar faces already," she said, her blue eyes smiling right at Charlotte.

That was the beginning of school, and after that the day whisked by. Despite looking so pale and quiet, Lucy—Miss Keator—was a very lively, firm sort of person. She kept the students in good order without being stern and, much to everyone's relief, without the use of whips or pointers. Charlotte loved her at once. She felt as if she had known Miss Keator a long time, although she had only met her that once. It seemed to Charlotte that she and Miss Keator somehow belonged to each other, because of who the teacher's sweetheart was. When Miss Keator smiled at Charlotte, the secret Charlotte read in her eyes was about Will.

At the noon recess, all the girls went to sit

beneath the school yard oaks to eat their dinners. They spread out their napkins in the shade and talked about Miss Keator. Most of them had never seen her before.

Charlotte did not want to tell them much. She did not want to hear anyone talk about Will. So she said simply that she had met Miss Keator once in town (which was quite true), and that she knew the teacher came from Dorchester.

Susan understood Charlotte's feelings without being told, as she always did. She did not say anything about Miss Keator being Will's sweetheart.

She only said, "She's awful sweet. I wish I didn't have to go away. I bet the Boston teachers always whip."

The other girls clucked in sympathy, for it was well known that Master Phelps came from Boston.

"Miss Keator *is* sweet," said the girl named Freda. "But my land, is she plain! We needn't fear that she'll go and get married on us. She's bound to be an old maid."

Charlotte's cheeks burned. "You watch your mouth!" she flashed. "You don't know anything, Freda Gregg!"

Charlotte jumped up and ran back into the schoolhouse, leaving her dinner tumbled on its napkin under the tree. Miss Keator was eating quietly at her desk. She looked up in some surprise when Charlotte burst in.

"Charlotte? Is anything the matter?" she asked, rising from her chair.

"No, miss," Charlotte murmured. She would die before telling Miss Keator what Freda Gregg had said.

"Are you sure?" Miss Keator came around her desk and sat down on the bench beside Charlotte.

Charlotte could not speak; she nodded her head vigorously. She felt Miss Keator's gaze upon her bent head.

"All right, dear. You know," said Miss Keator brightly, "I'm glad I'll get to know your family better, now I've moved to Roxbury. I always liked to hear Will's stories of the goings-on in your house."

Charlotte stared up at her teacher. "You did? Truly?" she asked.

"Truly." Miss Keator was about to say more, when Susan flew into the room. She had Charlotte's dinner basket and her own swinging from her arms.

"I told that Freda Gregg—" she was saying, and then she saw Miss Keator and her mouth snapped shut. "Oh!"

Miss Keator's eyes twinkled. "You're about to drop your cookies, dear," she said, pointing at the napkin gaping open on one of the baskets.

"Oh! That's Charlotte's," said Susan. She clutched at the napkin and handed the whole jumbled bundle to Charlotte. Miss Keator helped them spread the rest of their dinners out on the bench, and she said they just had time to finish eating before she must ring the bell.

All the rest of that day Charlotte was bursting inside with things she wanted to ask Miss Keator. She wanted to know if anybody had gone up north to get Will and bring him back, and how Will would travel if he had lost his leg like Lewis had lost his finger.

She wanted to know if Miss Keator thought Will was dead. At least, part of her wanted to. There was another part of Charlotte that was afraid to know.

Hello and Good-bye

Mama was eager to hear all about Miss Keator when Charlotte came home from school.

"Mrs. Waitt stopped in this mornin', she did," Mama said, stirring a batter of rye flour, eggs, and milk in her big mixing bowl. She was making fritters for supper, to go with the fried parsnips left over from dinner. "When she told me who the new teacher was, you could've knocked me over wi' a feather. It stands to reason, though. The Roxbury school is a fine catch for a young lady that needs to earn her livin'."

She sprinkled cinnamon and salt into the batter, and she took the tin nutmeg grater off its shelf over the kitchen hearth. Charlotte felt very happy to be back in her own nice kitchen. She had liked sitting beside Susan in Miss Keator's school all day, but it was lovely to be home again, with Lydia and Mary playing peek-eye in their favorite spot beneath the table, and Mama gossiping with Charlotte as if Charlotte were a grown-up lady.

"I think Miss Keator is awful nice, Mama," she said. To sound more grown-up, she added, "She keeps order quite well."

Mama's mouth twitched. "She does, does she? Well, it's glad I am to hear that. Canna have you lads and lassies runnin' wild in the schoolroom, can we?"

Charlotte agreed solemnly that no, indeed, they couldn't. Mama rubbed the little brown nutmeg over the sharp pointed holes of the grater, causing tiny brown flakes to sift into the bowl of batter. Charlotte leaned close to breathe in the spicy nutmeg scent. She thought there was nothing in the world that smelled as good as nutmeg—not even lilacs. Mama gave her the grater and the half-grated nut. She said that Charlotte might grate the rest into a little dish, if she liked, to be mixed with brown sugar and sprinkled on the hot fritters after they had been fried in a skillet.

"Did Miss Keator say where she's boardin', Lottie?" Mama asked.

Charlotte shook her head. But she had seen Miss Keator turn south on Centre Street, after school, and she told Mama so.

Mama looked thoughtful. "The Ben Chesters, mostly likely, or the Underwoods. It's a pity she didna think o' askin' us. I'd have been happy to board her. Though I suppose, if Will comes back . . ."

She trailed off. Charlotte hated when people did not finish their sentences. She always had the feeling that the part they left out was the most interesting part.

Papa and the boys came in, then, and Papa had a surprise.

"This'll please ye, Lottie," he said, with his hands hidden. "One o' me customers lacked the cash to settle his accounts today, but he paid me part in somethin' he picked up at the harbor yesterday."

He brought out from behind his back a fat round jug of real cane molasses. Lydia and Mary scrambled out from behind the table to see, and Charlotte jumped up and down. They had not had real molasses in over a year, as the war had made it hard to get.

Mama clapped her hands and said that was grand, they'd have it over their fritters for supper. She put the nutmeg-sugar Charlotte had mixed into a jar, to use another time.

Supper was a merry meal that night. All of them ate molasses until their mouths were sticky and their bellies ached. Afterward, Mama let Charlotte put the jug away in the sideboard in the space where the old molasses jug had gone, the dear old redware jug that Charlotte had thought of as the father in a little family of dishes. Now the slender vinegar-cruet mother had a new husband. Charlotte crouched on her heels and stared at the pair in the sideboard cabinet, trying to get accustomed to the new father jug. He was bigger than the old one, sturdy, not so jolly. The glaze on his stout red-brown body was very shiny. In the dark cupboard it had the glittery look of a cat's eyes peering out of a barn corner at night. Charlotte wasn't sure she liked this bold newcomer.

But she liked having molasses again, all right.

The school days flew by, and in a week's time Charlotte was fairly dazzled by all the things she had learned. Miss Keator had started all the girls on sewing samplers. (All, that is, except the very little ones, the noisy three-year-olds who sat on the center bench near the teacher's desk and scribbled on their older brothers' and sisters' slates.) She had told the girls to bring in squares of clean muslin from home, and any bits of thread their mothers could spare. Then she had stunned them all by giving them each a shiny, brand-new needle as a present. Not one girl in the school had ever had her own needle before—not her own never-before-used one, at least.

Miss Keator gave a needle to each of the older boys, too, though boys did not make samplers. She said a fellow never knew when he might need to stitch on a button, and she'd be pleased to teach any boy with sense enough to want to learn how.

Everyone was happy about those needles. But after a little while Miss Keator had to take most of the boys' needles back, to stop them from poking one another in the arms.

Charlotte worked hard on her sampler. Charlotte and Susan, in the first-grade class, were to begin their samplers with a line of running stitch across the top of the cloth square. Miss Keator showed them how to hold the pale fabric taut between their fingers and to pull the thread through with just the right amount of tug—not too weak so that the stitch was loose and untidy, nor with so much force that the cloth was drawn into a pucker. Charlotte had practiced a running stitch many times before, and Miss Keator said her neat line of stitches was a thing to be proud of. Charlotte felt glowing inside, like one of the buildings at the Illumination last winter. She liked the way that straight line of red-wool dashes looked against the creamy muslin, like a nice red road.

Some of the older girls had made samplers last year, in Miss Heath's school, and this year they were allowed to choose a short verse to embroider. Freda Gregg chose:

> *When I this little record see,*
> *I think how happy it would be,*
> *If Pa and Ma should live to say,*
> *Our children walk in wisdom's way.*

Charlotte and Susan whispered to each other about that verse as they bent over their samplers. They agreed that Freda had a long way to go to get to "wisdom's way." They were both still cross with her for calling Miss Keator an old maid.

All too soon it was Saturday, the end of the week. Susan said her mother wanted her to come home at the dinner recess. She had only let Susan go to school that morning so that she might say good-bye. Susan's father had gone ahead to Boston at daybreak with a wagonload of their belongings, and he was coming back to pick up Susan and Mrs. Custer and the baby that afternoon. Tonight Susan would sleep in her old room in the house her father owned near the wharves, and she would never come to the Roxbury school again.

Charlotte could not study her lessons that morning. The words were blurry in her reader. Miss Keator did not scold her, and she did not scold Susan for crying all through the arithmetic lesson. At noon, she called Susan to the front of the room and gave her a hug. She said they all would miss her, and the class sang, "For She's a Jolly Good Fellow." Susan sobbed and Charlotte cried. Even Freda Gregg cried, which made Charlotte mad. Freda wasn't losing her best friend.

When Miss Keator dismissed the class for

dinner, Charlotte and Susan ran outside to their favorite spot beneath a stand of birches on the hill beside the schoolhouse.

"I wish you could come visit me in Boston," said Susan mournfully.

"I wish I could, too."

They promised to write each other letters if they could get the postage money, and with a sudden notion that pleased them both immensely, they decided to trade the needles Miss Keator had given them. They took their folded-up samplers out of their apron pockets and broke the thread with their teeth as they had seen their mothers do. Solemnly, they made the exchange. Sunlight flashed off the slim silvery needles, making them wink their eyes. They were winking anyway, because both of them were crying again.

Then Susan turned and ran down the hill toward the street. She passed behind a screen of trees, so that Charlotte could not see her anymore.

The Smithy at Night

The bloom time passed, and the hot weeks came. Mama put a linen warp on her loom in a pattern of blue and white stripes to make a lightweight cloth for summer dresses. At night, after Lydia and Charlotte and Mary had been tucked into bed (for Mary, who had turned two in June, had never gone back to sleeping with Mama and Papa after Lewis got sick), Mama would sit at the loom late into the night, weaving.

The heavy wooden loom took up a full half

of the girls' bedchamber. There was nowhere else in the house where it would fit. It had solid oaken beams and heavy foot-treadles that made a *clunk* and a *squeak* when Mama pressed them. Charlotte liked falling asleep to those soft thumpings and creakings, and the *whisk-thunk* of Mama's shuttle sliding back and forth across the web, and the firm *thud* of the beater.

Charlotte would peek over the coverlet at Mama's dim figure swaying on the bench. The summer days were so long that the children were in bed before the sun had quite sunk below the treetops, and Mama left the bedroom shutters open a little so that she had light enough to work by. Sometimes the red-gold sun poured through the window and turned Mama's skin to gold. Charlotte would watch as long as she could, and when her eyes grew heavy she would close them and listen to the stories Mama told in the low ballads she sang as she worked. Her voice rippled softly like the murmur of a stream:

The Smithy at Night

"Her brow is like the snowdrift,
  Her neck is like the swan,
  Her face it is the fairest,
  That e'er the sun shone on,
  That e'er the sun shone on,
  And dark blue is her eye
  And for bonnie Annie Laurie,
  I'd lay me down and die.

"Like dew on the gowan lyin',
  Is the fall o' her fairy feet;
  And like winds in summer sighin'.
  Her voice is low and sweet;
  Her voice is low and sweet,
  She's all the world to me,
  And for bonnie Annie Laurie,
  I'd lay me down and die."

Then it would be morning, with Mama's voice soaring loud through the floorboards from the kitchen below:

"Come along, come along,
  Let us foot it all together,

Come along, come along,
Be it gay or stormy weather!"

And when Charlotte looked at the loom, there would be a few more inches of striped cloth rolled around the cloth beam.

Mama could weave at night because Papa was working late, too. He had so much work at the smithy that Mama said it would be a miracle if he didn't work himself into an early grave. All of them knew Papa could not wait much longer before hiring a new striker. He did not want to do it; he shook his head and turned away whenever the subject came up.

No one in the family wanted Papa to hire someone new. It would mean something too serious, too final, about Will. Papa had gone to Dorchester to see Will's parents, and they had said they'd had a letter from the hospital in Maine, telling them Will was gravely wounded and it was not yet known whether he would live or die. Since then, the Paysons had heard nothing. They had written more letters, but no one had answered. Mr. Payson said he aimed to go to Maine himself just as soon as he got his hay in. But that would not be for some weeks yet.

So Papa put off hiring a striker, and he worked at his forge half the night. Lewis stayed as late as Papa would allow him, helping. Lewis had grown tall in the past months, and his face had the same red, singed look Papa's had from spending so much time near the red-hot coals.

One night a mosquito got under the sheets and bit Charlotte so many times the itching woke her up. Mary was breathing heavily beside her, her hair pressed into damp flat rings against her cheek. On Mary's other side, Lydia was snoring. The loom was quiet, and the room was very dark.

Charlotte lay scratching her leg, listening to the quiet house. She thought she heard a noise in the distance, a clanging sound such as swords might make, crashing against each other. It scared her a little, and she got out of bed to find out what it was.

The narrow hallway was pitch black. She

wished she had a candle to go downstairs with. Instead she sat down and went down the stairs on her bottom, one step at a time. There were noises in the kitchen, not the frightening swordfight sound, but the safe gritty noise of feet sliding over the sand that coated the kitchen floorboards.

It was Mama, still in her daytime clothes, stirring something in a kettle as though it were the middle of the day. Beneath her brown skirt her bare feet poked out, and—Charlotte's breath caught when she saw—Mama's hair was long and loose, like a little girl's. She was not wearing the white cap that all grown-up ladies wore in the house, and she had unpinned the coil of hair from her neck. The long auburn waves shimmered in the hearthlight like the spun gold in one of Mama's fairy stories.

"Mama," Charlotte breathed, and Mama turned around in surprise.

"Lottie! Whatever are you doing up, lass!"

Charlotte shrugged. "I heard something. That—" She paused to listen, and they both heard it: the fearful ringing clangs.

Mama nodded. "Why, that's just your father, lass, in the shop. I'm amazed it hasna awakened you children before this."

Charlotte felt silly; she had been listening to Papa hammer iron her entire life. Surely she ought to have known the sound of that. But it sounded different, somehow, when you were only listening to it, when you could not see the hammer and the iron.

"I thought it was soldiers fighting," she told Mama. "With swords."

"Ah," said Mama. "I see. Well, if it's any comfort to you—and I dinna ken that it should be—nowadays soldiers do most o' their fightin' wi' guns, not swords. Anyhow, you needna worry about soldiers battlin' here. The war is over, and 'tis to be hoped there'll not be another one in our lifetime."

She straightened up, and her long hair swirled around her shoulders. Charlotte thought she had never seen anyone so beautiful.

"I wish you would wear your hair like that all the time, Mama," she said.

"Oh, you do, do you? A fine sight I'd be, doin' the marketin', in my bare feet and my hair hangin' wild!" Mama laughed, softly, so as not to waken the sleepers upstairs. "Come, lassie, as long as you're up you might as well help me carry a bit o' lunch to your father and your brother."

Charlotte giggled. Imagine eating a lunch in the middle of the night! Mama said the men worked up an appetite at night just the same as they did during the day—and besides, she said, food was the only thing she could get them to take a rest for.

Because it was so late at night, Mama didn't bother to put on her cap before going outside. The cool dark brushed at Charlotte's face. The air smelled salt and damp, for the breeze was coming off the marshes at the end of Tide Mill Lane. Charlotte held the plate of sausages Mama had given her close to her chest, shooing away the mosquitoes with an anxious hand.

The iron clanging was louder, and Charlotte wondered how anyone could sleep through this. Red light pulsed in the windows of the smithy. It did not look a bit like the Illumination; this was a fiery goblin light, not a golden glow. Charlotte hurried to keep close behind Mama as she went through the wide doors.

Papa and Lewis smiled to see them and gladly put down their tools. Their faces were streaked with soot and sweat. They said a teamster's axle had busted on the way through town, and they had promised to have it repaired by morning. Mama shook her head, frowning. She looked at Lewis critically and vowed that if he was going to stay up all night working then he'd better plan on sleeping through till noon the next day.

"Growin' lads need rest," she said firmly, when Lewis opened his mouth to protest.

"Papa," pleaded Lewis, but Papa shook his head.

"You must do as your mother says, lad. I'll save the heavy work for the afternoon."

Papa cleared off a stump of wood to use for a chair. Charlotte sat on Papa's knee while he wolfed down his sausage and bread. She knew she was getting soot on her nightgown, but it didn't matter. Papa's strong arm snuggled close against her back. Mama watched to be sure that Lewis ate every bite, and she made him drink a full tumbler of milk.

Moths beat against the windows outside and came fluttering into the smithy to hover around the forge. Charlotte heard the barn owl screeching somewhere from the direction of the garden, and all around the crickets chirped their steady song. Inside the smithy the air was warm as daylight. But outside the cool night breeze ruffled the maple leaves and made the tall grasses shudder. The red coals smoldered in the forge, waiting for Papa and Lewis to finish eating. They were as fiery red as Mama's hair, but not half so beautiful.

Rain on the Window

At last the summer rush eased up on Papa a little, and he was able to spend some evenings in the parlor with Mama and the others. He played checkers with Lewis, and he taught Tom how to play. Mama said he ought to teach the girls, too, so Papa took Charlotte on his knee and showed her how to slide the carved wooden disks from square to square. Charlotte liked checkers; it was a very tidy game, each little square so crisp and neat.

Lydia didn't care to learn checkers. Mama was teaching her to spin.

Papa closed the smithy for a couple of days (causing Mama to declare the world must be coming to an end) so that he and the boys could get the hay in. All over Roxbury it was haying time. The yellow hay shocks made bumps in the stubbly fields. The sky was blue and hot, and all the farmers prayed the fine weather would hold.

But one morning when Charlotte woke up, she heard rain drumming on the roof. It beat against the window. There was no light. Mary, rubbing her sleepy eyes, did not believe it was morning. She thought it must still be the middle of the night.

Charlotte and Lydia hurried to dress themselves and Mary. Quickly they made their beds and did their upstairs chores. They were in a rush to get downstairs and find out if Papa's hay was going to be ruined. If the hay was gone, the cows would go hungry next winter.

Mama's mouth was set in a straight line,

and her hand beat angrily around a mixing bowl. Charlotte and Lydia looked at each other, frightened for the cows and for Mama and Papa.

"Let's get breakfast on the table, girls," Mama said quietly. That was all the talking that happened until they were gathered around the parlor table and Papa said grace. Lewis and Lydia, Tom and Charlotte ate their pancakes carefully, trying to keep their forks from clattering on the plates. All the time the rain was beating, beating on the windows.

Papa could not go out to work, with the rain so heavy. He couldn't work in the fields, and he said there wasn't any point in opening up the smithy. No customers would venture out in such weather. He stood at the parlor window, staring out, stroking his chin with his hand.

Mama stalked around the house like an angry cat. She took out her broom and swept the parlor floor with a fierce vigor, as if she were trying to sweep the storm clouds out of the sky. She swept so hard that some of the broom straws broke and went skittering across the floorboards. Charlotte and Mary ran around picking them up and throwing them into the fire. None of the children quite knew what to do with themselves. Lewis watched the rain with Papa. Tom played with his Jacob's ladder, clapping the wooden blocks back and forth on their ribbons. Lydia complained that the noise was driving her mad, but Tom would not stop. Then Lydia went to sit as close beside Tom as she could get, and she sang loudly in his ear:

> *"Oats, peas, beans, and barley grows,*
> *Oats, peas, beans, and barley grows,*
> *How, you or I or nobody knows,*
> *How oats, pease, beans, and barley grows."*

Over and over she sang it, like the drumming of the rain.

"Mama!" Tom cried.

"Lydia," sighed Mama. She shook her head and looked around the room at all of them.

"Och, a fine happy bunch we are this day. Come, we're bein' foolish. Papa got half the hay in, and if the rest is lost we'll trust to Providence to see us through. Sure and we're in a better state that most o' the folks around here. Just think o' the John Heaths, with all their hay still in the field."

"It's comin' down harder now," said Papa, shaking his head at the window.

"Well, you'll not make it stop by starin' at it," scolded Mama. "Come, let's have a bit o' a game. What shall it be? Twenty Questions? Pinch, No Smiling?"

"Pinch, No Smiling!" cried Charlotte and Tom in unison.

"All right, then. Get in a circle. Lew, you come, too."

Eagerly Charlotte ran to take her place in the circle. Papa stood next to her on one side and Lydia was on the other. Mama said Papa must start, as he was oldest.

So Papa turned to Charlotte and ever so gently pinched the tip of her nose. Charlotte held herself as stiffly as a rail and tried not to laugh. She must not so much as smile, or she would have to pay a forfeit.

She did not break. Papa bowed to her, and Mama cheered. Then it was Charlotte's turn to pinch Lydia's nose, and so it went around the circle. Lydia pinched Tom's nose, and Tom bent to tweak Mary's. Of course Mary laughed right away. She was giggling before Tom touched her.

"Forfeit!" cried Lewis. "Mary must pay the forfeit!"

Mary clapped her hands and crowed, for she thought Lewis meant she had won. That set all of them laughing, and for the first time that morning Charlotte forgot about the rain.

"The forfeit shall be—a shoe," said Mama. "Come, Mary-my-lass, give Tommy your shoe."

She got the shoe off Mary's foot, and then it was Mary's turn to pinch. Mama crouched down beside her so Mary could reach. Mary squeezed Mama's nose with such solemn care that all the rest of them burst out laughing again, including Mama.

"Pay the forfeit, pay the forfeit!" they cried, shrieking with laughter.

The game went around the circle until everyone had been pinched. Then those who had lost their shoes had to perform a trick to get them back. Tom made Mary touch her toes, and Papa said Mama must hop around the parlor on one foot.

It was all so funny and absorbing that everyone jumped with surprise when the mantel clock struck eleven. Charlotte could hardly believe it was still morning—playing at games in the parlor had such an after-supper feel.

"Mercy, I must get dinner on," said Mama, and suddenly all of them were listening to the rain. It was drumming harder now, and the wind was howling.

The high spirits worked up by the game drained quickly away. Papa was once more standing at the window, shaking his head.

"Och, I dinna like the look o' this, Martha," he muttered. "Look how the trees are bendin'."

Charlotte and Lydia helped Mama make a hasty dinner of fried salt pork, stewed tomatoes, and pickled beets. Mama lit candles for the table, for she said the house was altogether too dark and gloomy. The wind hurled sheets of rain at the walls and windows, and the fire jumped high and low in the hearth. Charlotte had never heard such a terrible wind, moaning and whistling. She had never known rain to hammer at the house with such fury. She was glad of the candles and the oil lamps burning in the parlor.

Just as they were sitting down to eat, a crash rang out above their heads. Papa started from his chair and ran up the stairs.

"Bring a pail, Martha!" he called down. "We've lost a shingle over the lads' room!"

The wind was louder than ever, and the rain was like horses galloping overhead. Mama flew to the kitchen and clattered up the stairs with a bucket. Charlotte and the others left the table; they hurried to the stairs to see what had happened, but Mama ordered them back.

"Keep to the parlor, and stay away from the windows!" she cried. "Lewis, bring me some towels! And another bucket, lad, hurry!"

Charlotte, Tom, and Lydia looked at each other with wide, silent eyes. They had never known a storm like this before. Mama and Papa were yelling from the boys' room overhead; their voices sounded very far away. Something crashed outside, and Charlotte heard the cows bawling.

"Papa, the barn!" shouted Tom. Papa came downstairs, half soaked with rainwater. Streams of water ran down his hair and dripped onto the floor. Mama was just behind him with an armful of sopping towels.

"I must take another pail up to Lewis. The rain fills them up so fast we I don't know what we'll do. Lew, where are you goin'?"

Papa was already in the lean-to. "I must check the stock," he called, and then he was gone out into the howling storm, while Mama shouted after him.

"The blasted fool," she said. "He'll be struck by a branch, or drowned in this rain, I shouldna wonder. The animals can fend for themselves!" Her eyes met Charlotte's and saw at once how frightened Charlotte was.

"Och, listen to me, runnin' on at the mouth," Mama said hastily. "Dinna worrit yourself, Papa will be fine. This storm has me all a-jitter, that's all. Goodness, listen to that wind."

She called for Lewis to help her carry the big washtub upstairs, to go under the leak in the roof. But while they were upstairs there was another crash, and a screeching, ripping sound, and Mama's voice shrieked something at Lewis.

Lewis thundered down the stairs and called to the younger children.

"Come! We must go to the cellar! Mama said so!"

"Where's Mama?" Charlotte wailed. She was half afraid the winds would pick Mama up and carry her away like a leaf or a corn husk.

"She's all right, she's coming," Lewis assured her. "Go on, get down to the cellar!"

The cellar stairs were behind a door in the kitchen. Charlotte hesitated at the top, not wanting to enter the pitch blackness that yawned up at her. There was no time to go back for a candle; Lewis was urging her on.

They all felt their way down the stairs and huddled together at the bottom. The storm's noise was fainter here, but still it was mighty. On the other side of the root cellar, the terrible wind rattled the wooden doors that led directly outside. The smells of potatoes and apples and onions were very strong. Charlotte's stomach felt queasy, from smelling things to eat when eating was the last thing on her mind.

"Hush, Mary, hush, Mary," Lydia kept repeating, for Mary was calling out for Mama.

"She's all right, Lydia," said Lewis, "leave her be."

It seemed to Charlotte that the storm would never cease; it would rage on and on forever above them, and Mama and Papa would never come. She swallowed hard against the tears in her throat. She mustn't frighten Mary. Groping in the darkness, she found Tom's hand. He squeezed her hand tight and did not let go. Charlotte loved him very much just then, for holding on so tight.

The Hurricane

All at once, Mama came clattering down the cellar stairs, an oil lamp burning in her hands. Her cap was dangling by its strings, and her hair had fallen in stringy, dripping locks across her face. Charlotte rushed at her—all of them did—and threw her hands around Mama's waist. Mama's skirt felt wet and heavy against Charlotte's face.

"Careful!" Mama cried out. "Mind the lamp!" She pushed them back a little and moved away from the stairs. Charlotte felt mud beneath her feet where Mama was dripping on the hard-packed earth of the floor.

Lydia was crying. "I thought you'd never come! Why didn't you come?"

"Whisht," said Mama, "I'm here now. What, d'you think I'd leave you down here in the dark? I was tryin' to save what I could from the boys' room. We lost part o' the roof there, and I fear 'twill be quite a flood."

"What's happening, Mama?" whispered Charlotte.

"It's only a storm, lass—aye, the worst one I ever saw. It'll be over soon."

She said the storm was called a hurricane, and it must have blown in from the sea.

How long they sat there, watching the shadows flicker on the faces in the lamplight, Charlotte didn't know. The cellar's thick walls muffled the sound of the wind, but still the faint keening went on, and a distant banging and hammering, as if the rain were pounding on the door, begging to be let in. Charlotte felt sick with worry over Papa. Mama said he would be fine; he was safe in the barn, and a stouter, stronger building there wasn't in all of Roxbury.

"Only think how glad the cows and sheep will be to have him there," Mama said.

"Poor things," said Lydia. "I wish I could go stay with them. I'm glad Papa's there."

To take their minds off their worry, Mama told them a story. She said the rain had made her think of it.

Mama's Story of the Good Housewife's Wish

Once on a time, there was a crofter and his wife who lived in a glen at the foot o' a green hill. The hill was called Tiree-top, and 'twas known that fairies lived there.

The crofter and his wife had a snug wee cottage and a fine piece o' land. Things went along well enough for them until the summer a drought fell upon the land. Now, mind you, this was Scotland, where a little rain falls sweetly nearly every day. When the crofter and his wife had seen a week go by with nary a drop o' rain, they were a wee bit worried. When a second week had gone by and no rain, they were a good deal worried. And when a third week had passed and still not so much as a thimbleful o' rain had fallen from the sky, they were terrible worried indeed. Their oats and barley were witherin' in the fields, and their rye was brown as wood.

"Och," said the good housewife, wringin' her hands, "sure and I wish it would rain— aye, rain and never stop!"

Well, as you might guess, that was a foolish thing to wish—standin', as she was, in the shadow o' a fairy mound. It was no more than a half a moment later that a great black storm cloud rolled into the sky, and the drops o' rain began to fall. Plump, heavy raindrops they were, and they went from a trickle to a downpour in no time at all. The crofter and his good wife, they were that overjoyed they didna run for cover but instead danced about madcap in the rain.

It rained and it rained. After a while, they went drippin' into the cottage and watched from the windows as the rain poured down. They watched a long time, for that rain, it didna stop fallin'. A day, and another day, and another, and still the rain streamed down.

Now the crofter and his wife began to worry in the other direction. Every farmer kens that too much rain is as bad as too little. They began once more to wring their hands and bite their lips. It seemed as if their crops were bound to be ruined one way or t'other.

On the evenin' o' the third day o' solid drenchin' rain, a knock came at the cottage door. The good housewife, she opened it, and what did she see standin' there but a wee slip o' a woman, all dressed in green.

"I've come to take shelter from the storm," she said. "My home 'neath the hillside is drippin' at the seams."

Then the good housewife kenned the auld woman was one o' the fairy folk, and her eyes opened wide.

"Come in, come in," she said hastily, and she took the auld woman's wet mantle and led her to a seat by the fire. The fairy woman toasted her wet feet and warmed her hands. Just as the crofter's wife was seein' her settled with a mug o' ale and a plate o' fresh-baked bannocks, there came another knock at the door.

This time 'twas the crofter who opened it, and he found himself starin' at three wee green-clad men, with long wet beards and rain drippin' off their noses.

"We've come," they said, "to take shelter from the storm."

And once more the good housewife bustled about, settlin' her guests at the fire with linen towels about their shoulders and food and drink in their hands. The fairies asked for honey to spread upon their bannocks, and cheese to cut the sweetness, and fruit and nuts to go with the cheese. The housewife scurried to and fro until she was quite worn out and her larder was half empty.

And so it went, more knocks upon the door and more drippin' wet fairy folk seekin' shelter from the rain. Young ones, auld ones, fairy mothers with babes squallin' in their arms. The wee cottage, it grew quite crowded, and the good housewife, she wondered if she had food and drink enough to serve such a crowd. Already she was down to her last wheel o' cheese.

"Just a drop o' drink to wet my lips," one of them would cry, wavin' an empty ale-stoup in the air, or "If only I had a bite more to eat, how happy I would be!"

The crofter had to open his last keg o' ale, and the good housewife found herself scrapin' the bottom o' the flour barrel.

"What shall we do?" they asked each other. "Och, if only the rain would stop!"

At that, the noisy fairy host fell silent, and they all of them looked at the wife.

"You ought not complain about what you asked for in the first place," reproached the wee auld woman who had come first to their door. And all the fairy folk nodded their heads wisely.

Then the good housewife understood that it was her own wish that had brought this never-endin' rain.

"Do ye mean to say," she whispered, "that this rain will nivver stop fallin?"

"Why should it?" declared the fairy crone. "Sure and we're happy where we are. Such a nice cozy house, and the rain drummin' so pleasantly on the roof. Och, but dinna ye fret, dear—I expect we'll grow weary o' it after a hundred years or so."

The crofter and his wife, their blood ran cold. A hundred years!

"Ah, yes," added the auld fairy, "if only I had another o' your delicious bannocks, I'd be content to sit here another thousand years."

A drop of hope sprung forth in the wife's breast.

"Forgive me," she murmured, "but I fear

my flour has run out. It's terrible sorry I am that I have no more victuals to serve ye."

The fairies laughed, and the wee auld woman told the housewife not to worry.

"Ye ought to have said somethin' before this," she cackled. "I can fill a flour barrel as easy as winkin' an eye. Go and look."

The wife and her husband flew to the flour barrel, and sure enough, it was full up again! They looked in the larder, and they found a nice yellow cheese lyin' on the shelf just as pretty as you please, and the honey jar full to the brim with lovely golden honey. The crofter ran to check the ale barrel, and it, too, was full once more.

"More! More!" the fairies called, waving their empty mugs in the air and clatterin' their knives upon their plates. Och, how the wife and her husband had to fly about after that, fillin' mugs and fryin' bannocks and slicin' the wedges o' cheese. No matter how much cheese the wife served her hungry visitors, there was always some left; and no matter how much flour she scooped out, the barrel was always full.

The wife and her husband could see that this might go on forever. The food would never run out, the rain would never stop fallin', and the fairies would never wish to leave.

A thought came into the wife's head. Happen the thing to do was to make her guests a wee bit less comfortable. She had always prided herself on her good cookin', but now she wondered if being too fine a cook could be a dangerous thing.

She set to mixin' up another mess o' bannocks. But this time, instead o' a pinch o' salt as she always used, she put in a great heapin' cupful. For good measure, she let the bannocks burn a little when she fried them up.

Then she sliced up more o' the cheese. She took a lump o' soap out o' the cupboard, and she rubbed it all over the cheese. She stirred vinegar into the honey, and she whispered to her husband to mix some whey in with the ale.

She went quickly around the cottage servin' the new bannocks and honey and cheese. While the fairies were takin' their first bites, the housewife quietly slipped a wet peat onto the fire.

"Faugh!" the fairies cried, wrinklin' their noses. They spit out their mouthfuls and declared the bannocks were the worst they'd ivver tasted, and they said the cheese and the honey were worse than the bread.

"Ale, ale!" they cried. "Ye must give us somethin' to wash away the taste!"

So the good housewife filled up their mugs o' ale, and each and every one o' the fairies drank deep. Then they burst out sputterin', for the ale was the worst tastin' of all.

By then the fire had begun to smoke, and the fairies eyes were stingin' and smartin'. They all jumped up and ran for the door, and they hurried out into the rain.

"We'll want a bit o' fine weather to dry

out our house," said the auld fairy woman crossly, and—snap!—just like that, the rain stopped fallin'. The sun broke out from behind the black clouds, and the crofter's fields sparkled in the golden light. With not so much as a "fare you well," the fairies raced one and all up the green slope to a door cut into the side of Tiree-top Hill. The door closed behind them, and that was the last the crofter and his wife saw of their fairy neighbors.

But the fairies left somethin' behind, for they had forgotten to take away the magic that kept the flour barrel from emptyin' and the ale from runnin' dry. The honey jar stayed ever full of the sweetest clover honey, and as for the cheese—why, the crofter's great-great-grandchildren are still eatin' it today.

"I wish I had some," said Tom when the story was over. "I'm awful hungry."

"Hush," said Mama, "listen."

The rain was easing up. Its drumbeat upon

the outside cellar doors was no longer so violent, and the wind had quieted. Charlotte had not noticed when the terrible pounding noise had stopped, but it seemed to her now that it had been gone a long time.

"Can we go up, Mama?" she asked, and Mama nodded and said she would go first, to make sure it was safe.

She left the lamp with Lewis and went upstairs. In a moment she was back, and she said they might all come up.

Charlotte ran up the stairs as fast as she could go. It felt wonderful to come out of the dark stuffy cellar into the kitchen, where the air was fresh and cool. But the kitchen was strangely dark, darker even than the rain, which was still halfheartedly drumming, ought to make it.

"Papa boarded up the windows," said Mama, her voice rather clipped. "To save the glass from breakin'."

That was the pounding noise Charlotte had heard—it had been Papa, hammering boards over the windows from outside. She had been afraid of the hammering, when really it had been Papa all along.

"The worst o' it is past," said Mama. "I wonder how Papa made out, in the barn."

After the Storm

Papa was all right. He came in from the barn, thoroughly wet and smelling of cow. His breeches were smeared with mud and grime.

"The stock'll be all right, now the wind's quit. The sheep and Mollie didna mind so much, but Patience was mighty spooked. She took to kickin' at the wall, until I thought she was goin' to bring the whole barn down around us."

"When did you board the windows?" Mama asked, and now her eyes were flashing. "I'd have come out to help you, you fool, if I'd known."

Papa smiled a little. "That's why I didna tell ye. Nae sense in both o' us gettin' soaked to the bone."

"You might have been hit on the head by a branch, Lew, and then where would we be?" Now that the hurricane was over, Mama was angry. She said Papa ought not to have risked his neck that way, nor left the animals alone.

"Now then, Martha," said Papa lightly. "I think we've seen enough storms for one day."

His eyes twinkled at Mama, and she burst out laughing. "All right. I suppose all's well that ends well."

It seemed strange to Charlotte that Mama could say all was well. The upstairs was a terrible mess; Tom and Lewis's room was swimming in water, their furniture ruined. Water had spilled through the floorboards and doused the parlor in places; Mama's workbasket was a puddle of water, and the hooked rug squished when Charlotte stepped on it. The pretty wallpaper, with its pale blue stripes, was a soggy, bubbled mess on the west wall.

Papa left the windows boarded till the next day. He had not been able to board the upstairs windows, of course, and Mama said it was providential that there had been no damage at all in the girls' bedchamber. The old loom was fine, and Tom and Lewis's mattresses were saved because Mama had thrown them on the girls' bed.

Tom and Lewis slept on the floor of the girls' room that night, on their own mattresses. Mama and Papa slept in their own bed in the parlor, for they had rolled up the rug and sopped up all the water. Their quilt had been soaked at the edges, where it touched the floor, but the mattress was all right.

The next day was Sunday. They all went outside early in the morning to see what the storm had done. The bright sun made Charlotte blink. The world was glistening wet and streaked with mud. All around, the ground was littered with leaves and branches.

There were other things, too, things the wind had carried from far away and dropped on their land. Charlotte found a milk pail in the dooryard; it was not one of Mama's. Lewis plucked a man's red underwear out of the maple tree.

That was easy to do, because the maple was lying on its side in the yard. Tears came to Mama's eyes when she saw it. She had loved that tree. The storm had torn it up, roots and all, as if it were a weed.

"I suppose it's a mercy it didna fall on the house," said Mama, but her voice was very sad.

Charlotte felt like crying, too, when she saw the herb garden—the rosemary bush and the lavender had been uprooted and flung into the muddy soup that had once been a neatly raked plot. Most of the perennials were wind shredded or drowned. The little plum tree that had shaded the garden wall was gone altogether. Charlotte and Lydia looked all over the garden and the field beyond, but they never did find that tree.

"How could a storm carry off a whole tree?" Charlotte asked Mama.

"That storm was powerful enough to carry *you* off, if you'd been caught out in it," said Mama. Charlotte shivered and felt for a moment like running back inside.

Little rivulets and streams of water coursed everywhere around them. The barnyard had become a small pond. Two of Mama's hens had drowned. Lydia wept bitterly at the sight of their poor waterlogged bodies lying half swallowed by the mud.

The cows bawled anxiously from the barn. Papa and Mama went in to milk them; the milking must go on just as usual, though the whole world was different today. Charlotte helped Lydia feed the chickens. Their round yellow-rimmed eyes seemed to glare at the girls as if they were to blame for the loss of their friends. Lydia gave them extra grain, to make up for all they had suffered.

After a while Mama said they had best get inside and eat some breakfast. But Papa said he would eat later; he wanted to walk over to the town common to see how bad the damage was there. Mama nodded and gave him a large hunk of bread and a wedge of cheese to eat as he walked.

Breakfast was a gloomy, hurried meal—just some cold leftover beans and bread and cheese, which Charlotte and the other children ate as quickly as they could. Papa had not yet had a chance to take the boards off the windows, and none of them could bear to stay long inside the dark house.

Papa came home after a while, shaking his head. The damage was terrible, he said. He had talked to Mr. Heath and some of the other men in town. All the hay that had been left shocked in the fields—all of it was gone. Any crops that had not yet been harvested were drowned or washed away. The apple harvest had just been getting underway. There would be few apples for drying this year, he told Mama sadly.

"Cider'll be cheap, though, wi' so many windfalls."

He said the storm had uprooted trees,

blown down fences, and torn off roofs all over town. Several families had lost entire buildings—Mr. Abner Davis, Papa said, had lost both his sheds, all his hay, and both of the chimneys on his house.

"Not just that," said Papa, "his barn was moved clean off its foundation. John Heath saw it wi' his own eyes—said it was five feet if it was an inch."

"We're lucky our own roof held," said Mama. "And the smithy was all right?"

"Aye, those walls are so stout it'd take a storm twice as strong as that one to knock them over."

"Dinna speak that way," Mama scolded, shuddering. "I hope I never see a storm like that one again in all my life. It's a wonder no one was killed."

"How can you say that, Mama?" cried Lydia. "The poor hens!"

"Aye," said Papa. "But nae people, and that's somethin' to be thankful for."

It was a strange day; there was so much work to do, and not much of it could be done because it was Sunday. There could be no church that day—the storm had taken off part of the meetinghouse roof. Papa said he reckoned the good Lord wouldn't mind if he uncovered the windows at least, and once the boards had been pried off, everyone felt much better. The late-morning sun poured cheerily through the windows as if it were quite an ordinary day.

Papa took the big Bible from its place on the little low round table beside Mama's chair. She kept her workbasket right next to that table, and everyone agreed it was a miracle that the Bible had not been touched by so much as a droplet of water, when the workbasket and everything in it were ruined. They all gathered around Papa, and he read them the story of Noah and his ark. Mama chuckled softly and said she supposed they would all understand that story much better now.

Later, Papa took all the children but Mary down Tide Mill Lane toward the flats, to see how high the water had risen. The flats were flooded, a wide gray blue ocean of shrieking, wheeling birds. The wind gusted across the water, and on the distant shore the buildings of Boston stood pale and quiet.

"Look, the gulls dinna ken what to do," said Papa. "The rocks they're used to are underwater."

At the water's edge, the gray and white gulls rose into the sky with clams in their beaks. They flapped around the soggy new shoreline, looking for a stony surface upon which to crack open the clamshells. Now and then a bird would let a clam fall upon the soft mud, but the shells only bounced and did not break open. The poor gulls could not open their dinners that day.

"I should think they'd go fishing instead," said Lewis. "Bound to be a good catch today."

Back at home there were visitors—neighbors, the Waitts, who had dropped by to see that everyone was all right. Mama and Papa compared stories, and Mama jumped up to fill a basket for a family who was said to have been flooded out of their house.

"They're living in the barn," said Mrs. Waitt. "I told Eveline they ought to come stay with us, but she wouldn't hear of it."

All that day and the next, the neighbors came calling. They stood in the dooryard with Mama and Papa and shook their heads over what the storm had done. They all wore the same faces and said the same things. Charlotte grew so used to seeing visitors come down the lane that she stopped paying them any mind. She and Tom were poking into the puddles with sticks, to see if the wind had dropped anything interesting in them. Tom had found an apple, mouthwateringly red and perfect skinned, without a single bruise. Charlotte turned up a most remarkable treasure—a muddy silver coin—a five-cent piece! But Tom thought it had most likely been there before the storm.

Charlotte ran to show Mama and Papa, and she nearly collided with a man coming slowly up the lane. She thought at first he was a very old man, because he walked with a cane, in short hobbling steps. Then she saw the man's face, and she was so surprised that she fell down, hard, in the mud.

The man was Will.

He leaned on his cane and reached out a hand toward her. His face was different, tanned and lined and thin, and yet somehow he was just exactly the same. His wavy hair was tumbled on his forehead; his eyes smiled at her as they had always done.

"I *knew* you'd come home," said Charlotte, taking his hand.

Will helped her to her feet, wincing a little as he pulled. He grinned at her and said, "Hullo, Charlotte. How's our towhee?"

"She came back in the spring, just as you said!" Charlotte told him. She was happy in all her bones, so happy that she could not stop talking. "She had five eggs, but only four of them hatched, and Mama said the babies made more noise than a dozen Marys—which would be very noisy indeed, if you ask me—"

She got no further, because by then the rest of the family had noticed Will, and they

crowded around him, hugging and squeezing and slapping him on the back, until he laughed and said they ought to show a little more respect for an old war veteran like himself. Mama was laughing and crying all at once, and Papa's eyes glistened. Lewis grinned so wide Mama said the two corners of his mouth were bound to meet in the back of his head. Lydia came running with Mary by the hand. Will whistled at the sight of Mary and said that this great, galloping little girl could not possibly be the baby he had said good-bye to last year. Mary didn't remember Will at all, and she hid her face in Lydia's skirt.

"All of you," said Will. "You've grown up so much. I feel like I've been gone ten years instead of just the one."

"Och, lad, it's that good to see you I fear my heart will burst," said Mama tenderly, touching Will's sleeve. "Are you back to stay?"

"If Mr. Tucker will have me," said Will, his eyes suddenly serious. He raised the left leg of his trousers and knocked his shin with his cane. Charlotte heard a crisp rapping sound, like two sticks clapped together. Where Will's leg ought to have been, there was a fat, round stick of wood.

"You have a wooden leg?" asked Tom, his eyes wide with awe. Charlotte had heard of wooden legs, but she had never seen one. She listened quietly while Will told how the doctors had had to take off his leg at the knee, after he was shot. He hiked up his trousers to show how the wooden leg was fastened to a sort of leather cup, which fit around his knee. The leather cup had straps that were tied around the upper part of his leg, the part that had been left by the doctors.

Charlotte felt shy, hearing all this and looking at the wooden leg. She studied Will's face instead, and again she saw that he was the same Will Payson she had known half her life. She supposed Will was right; Mary had changed more in the past year than he had, except for his leg. Charlotte still thought of Mary as a baby, but she was big enough to run now, and jump, and talk, and play with dolls instead of tearing them apart.

After the Storm

Lewis showed Will his hand with the missing finger. Will pursed his lips and whistled again, and he said he'd seen many a fellow in the camp hospital with the same sort of injury. Lewis looked almost proud, and Tom asked if he could try to walk with Will's cane.

"Mercy," said Mama suddenly, "I dinna ken what's the matter wi' us. Standin' out here in the mud, runnin' our mouths while Will's most likely starvin' to death. Come inside, lad, and let me get you a bite to eat."

They trooped about him into the kitchen, and everyone scrambled to offer Will the best chair. He laughed and said they'd spoil him, for sure.

"Don't you know you're supposed to beat the hired help, and feed me on bread and water?"

"Whisht, lad, nivver a word of that," said Papa. "You're family."

Mama served him bread spread a half inch thick with butter, and cheese and cold sliced beef. Tom produced the apple he had found

253

in the yard, washed clean and rubbed until it shone.

"Dinna tell me you walked all the way from Dorchester?" asked Mama.

"No, I came on horseback with my father. His old auntie lives in Roxbury, you know, a widow. He wanted to see that she came through the storm all right. He dropped me on Washington Street; I told him if I could walk halfway home from Portland, I could manage a stone's throw to your place."

"You walked from Maine, then? With that leg?" Mama demanded.

"Wasn't so bad. I got lifts quite a bit along the way. I was just so glad to be walking—for a while there I thought I'd never be out of bed again."

His voice dropped low, and he told them about the fighting in Maine, the raid the British soldiers had made upon his camp. He had spent weeks in the hospital, half the time out of his head with fever, and when he had finally come out of it, his leg had been gone.

"The funny thing is, the war'd been over a month already when I took the wound. Word travels so slow, we didn't know it yet, and neither did the redcoats."

Sitting on a little stool beside him, Charlotte listened to Will and looked at the round end of the wooden leg resting on the floor. She tried to think what she had been doing at the time Will was shot. Perhaps she had been playing with Lydia or making a bed or helping Mama cook.

She remembered putting the cinnamon in the fritter batter on the first day of school. She shouted out suddenly, "Will! I know Miss Keator!"

Will smiled, and he said, "Well, I hope you're not too much in the habit of calling her that. I aim to make her Mrs. Payson before too long."

Then Mama cheered, and Papa laid his hand upon Will's thin shoulder. Lydia clasped her hands together and asked when the wedding would be, and would there be raisins or currants in the cake, or both?

Will chortled, cradling his face in his hands. "Go easy on me, dear, I've not been home a week yet. There's still a great deal to sort out."

He turned to Papa and said he hoped he'd be able to do his old job just as well as ever. "I'll be blunt with you, Mr. Tucker," he said soberly. "I think I can manage just about everything but the heaviest work. I'm still trying to get my balance back. The detail work, I reckon I can do just fine. And there's no mistaking I need the job badly. I saved every penny of my militia pay and the better part of the wages you paid me before that. I've got just about enough to buy a little plot of land and house lumber. But if I'm to marry Lucy, I'll need a job to put bread on her table. I was hoping you'd take me back on a trial basis, like, and we can see if I'll work out. If not, I'll look for counter work somewhere. But I don't want to settle Lucy in a house until I know one way or the other."

Mama opened her mouth to answer him, and Charlotte could see by the fire in her eyes that she was going to scold Will for even suggesting that he might not be fit to keep his job in Papa's shop. But Papa slipped a word in before she had a chance to speak; he nodded and said quietly, "Aye, that suits me fine. I've no doubt 'twill all work out."

Then Papa glanced at Mama. "Or else me wife," he added with a wink, "will have both our hides."

Will let out a long breath and leaned back in his chair, rubbing a litle at the place where his wooden leg met the knee. He felt Charlotte looking at him and smiled at her. All at once the great excitement of that day came rushing upon Charlotte, and she felt— she didn't know how she felt. She thought of how Mama had both laughed and cried when she saw Will outside the house. She thought of the wind, how it had howled around them last night like a pack of wolves, and how the rain had beat upon the walls; and she thought of the sun, shining this morning as if nothing at all had happened.

She thought of the bells that had pealed

across the flats last winter, when the war ended—that ringing, chiming, jubilant song. *That* was how she felt, and if she had a thousand bells to ring, they couldn't ring out loud enough.

Come Home to
Little House

The MARTHA *Years*
By Melissa Wiley
Illustrated by Renée Graef

The CHARLOTTE *Years*
By Melissa Wiley
Illustrated by Dan Andreasen

The CAROLINE *Years*
By Maria D. Wilkes
Illustrated by Dan Andreasen

The LAURA *Years*
By Laura Ingalls Wilder
Illustrated by Garth Williams

The ROSE *Years*
By Roger Lea MacBride
Illustrated by Dan Andreasen
& David Gilleece